AN ALLUSIVE LOVE

A MacNaughton Castle Romance
Book Two

By

Aubrey Wynne

ARE YOU SIGNED UP FOR DRAGONBLADE'S BLOG?

You'll get the latest news and information on exclusive giveaways, exclusive excerpts, coming releases, sales, free books, cover reveals and more.

Check out our complete list of authors, too!

No spam, no junk. That's a promise!

Sign Up Here

www.dragonbladepublishing.com

Dearest Reader;

Thank you for your support of a small press. At Dragonblade Publishing, we strive to bring you the highest quality Historical Romance from the some of the best authors in the business. Without your support, there is no 'us', so we sincerely hope you adore these stories and find some new favorite authors along the way.

Happy Reading!

CEO, Dragonblade Publishing

Additional Dragonblade books by Author Aubrey Wynne

A MacNaughton Castle Romance

Deception and Desire (Book 1)
An Allusive Love (Book 2)
A Bonny Pretender (Book 3)
A Merry MacNaughton Mishap (Novella)

PROLOGUE

A Lass in Love

Late Summer 1810
MacNaughton Castle

"WHAT DO YE mean she canna be my best friend?" shouted Brodie MacNaughton from the clifftop. "I thought ye were fond of Kirstine?"

His eyes focused on the kaleidoscope of color below as a waterfall tumbled into the clear blue loch. "MacNaughton blue," others had nicknamed the shade, after the clan's dominant eye color. The late afternoon sun peeked out from behind a cloud and created a rainbow from the cascade of sparkling drops.

"She's a lass, ye *eejit*." His older brother, Ian, climbed up the rock and slapped him lightly on the side of the head.

"Then why do ye claim that Lissie is yers?" He clenched his fists, tired of arguing with his smug brother. It wasn't in his nature to be on the offensive, but this point rankled him for some unknown reason.

"Because we're betrothed by our clans and bonded by our souls," Ian explained in a slow, patient manner that made Brodie want to thump him. "She's different, ye ken, she'll be my wife someday. Do ye plan to marry Kirstine?"

Brodie's jaw clamped tight. The rare tick of frustration surprised him. "For the love of saints, I'm no' thinking of marriage at all."

"Ye'll be ten and four soon. And yer eyes are already rove over the lasses. I saw ye spy the bonny redhead when we were in Glasgow." Ian chortled, a smug laugh that poked at Brodie's anger again.

"What does that have to do with Kirsty being my best friend?"

"There'll come a time when ye have to decide on a wife. Ye canna be betrothed to one and keep the other as yer confidante." Ian began the climb down the side of the hill. "Are ye coming or no'?"

"Aye," he said as he followed his brother sideways down the hill, grabbing at an occasional boulder or bush to keep his balance. "Ye say a wife willna appreciate my friendship with Kirstine?"

"Now ye're catching on, ye dunderhead," agreed Ian. He jumped the last few feet and pulled off his shirt, shoes, stockings and finally his kilt. Laying them all on a boulder, he climbed on top of it and pumped his fist in the air. "It's a braw day for a swim."

Brodie laughed as Ian yelled the MacNaughton war cry and jumped into the loch, his bare buttocks pale against the sun.

"Weel, a woman who canna accept Kirsty will never meet me at the church door." He copied Ian, but just as he was about to jump, he paused and peered over his shoulder. With a smile, he winked at a copse of trees. "*Fraoch Eilean!*" Brodie shouted to the echoing pines as he joined his brother in the cool water.

⁂

KIRSTINE WATCHED FROM their secret place in the woods. The pungent odor of pine, decayed wood, and leaves filled her nostrils as she brushed bits of dirt from her damp skirt. She'd been collecting herbs for her mother and heard the boys' conversation. She hadn't meant to eavesdrop, had intended to join them, in fact, until she heard her name. Instead, she crept to the place where they always met. Brodie's meditating spot. There was a plaid tucked in the branch above her, wrapped in oilskin. They often sat on it, eating a cold pasty, while Kirstine listened to Brodie's latest woes or comical stories.

Now she listened to him argue with his older brother. Ian was both right and wrong. They *were* the best of friends. *Aye, and so much more*, her heart whispered. Someday, the big oaf would see it. She swiped at the tear, then smiled. Brodie sensed her as he always did. He looked in her direction—his young stocky body already muscular from physical labor and hard play, his firm white cheeks bare and flexing—and winked at her. Her breath caught before a giggle bubbled up her throat.

She watched his wet, black hair catch the sunlight, streaks of blue rippling through the thick locks as he came to the surface and pushed it back from his face with both hands. She sighed. Her body was changing, and with it, her feelings for Brodie grew stronger. Emotions wreaked havoc on her mind, especially during her menses. When he touched her, leaned over her, or gave her a wink, her stomach tumbled. Her heart raced when he looked over her shoulder, his breath warm on her ear. Ma called it a sure sign she was smitten.

Kirstine knew better. This was no infatuation. At the age of thirteen, she was undeniably in love with Brodie. But he was in love with life and everyone in it. A favorite within his family and the neighboring clans. She realized she'd always have to share when it came to Brodie, his affections, his time. That was one of the things she loved about him. His exuberance, his excitement, his ability to pull her along on his grand adventures.

He had a new pet in the stable every spring, could never decide on a pup from his grandfather's deerhound litters, and always changed his mind about his favorite food.

"He's as fickle as the Highland weather," her mother had warned. "He'll break a score of hearts before he learns the pain himself."

Kirstine didn't see him as inconstant, but rather so full of energy and affection that his mind never quit whirling. He hated to sit and be idle. He was loyal—to the clan, to her, and to his own principles. If Brodie made a promise, he kept it. How could *that* be fickle?

Besides, his whims always passed, and then he came back to her. It was Kirstine he sought when he needed to work something through, or rant about his brothers or sister, or wonder about the ways of the world. It was Kirstine who comforted him when the rare disappointment dulled his enthusiasm. *She* was his constant, the shoulder he leaned on. Patience would be the key to his love. He would come to her eventually, as a man comes to a woman, and she would be waiting.

For life without Brodie MacNaughton was unthinkable.

CHAPTER ONE

A Twist in the Road

Late April 1819
Scottish Highlands

S CRATCHING AT HIS chest, Brodie poked his face under his plaid and inhaled. His nose wrinkled. He needed a bath. Desperately. He'd report to his grandfather, the MacNaughton, then find Kirstine. He'd had a conversation with his oldest brother, Lachlan, about the future clan chief. They had a plan, and he needed to think it through aloud with Kirsty.

As he emerged from a copse of trees, a movement to his right caught his eye. A long slope of spring grass gave way to another path that led to the village of Dunderave. He pulled up his horse and leaned over its neck to get a better look below.

A flash of red and blue jumped into his vision, disappeared, followed by a screech and the *clip clop* of horse hooves. Brodie nudged the gelding's sides with his heels and guided it down the hill. He came across a basket, partially filled with plants, then a wool shawl in the MacDunn tartan. At the bottom, in a shallow gully, lay a tangle of skirts and plaid, and a cursing girl. A dapple-gray pony stood on the other side of the path, sedately munching on grass.

"Weel, what do we have here?" Brodie grinned. "Are ye in need of some help, my bonny lass, or just need a wee rest?"

Kirstine pushed up on her elbows, kicked at her skirts, and righted her plaid. Somewhat. She blew the deep red locks from her eyes and squinted up at him. "Look who has come home. My brawny Brodie to the rescue." She smiled, dark eyes lit with pleasure as she held out a hand.

He slid from the saddle, then grasped her fingers, and pulled her to her feet. "The pony doesna like ye?"

"He's young and still a wee green. A hare dashed out in front of him, and he spooked." She brushed off her backside, then stood on tiptoe to kiss his cheek. "I was daydreaming instead of paying attention. On yer way home, then?"

He nodded and bent to help her collect the herbs that had spilled from her basket. Kirstine's mother was the clan's healer and sent her daughter out regularly to replenish medicinal supplies.

"What were ye dreaming about?" He retrieved the shawl that had been draped over her hair.

"None of yer business," she replied with a smirk, then picked up her skirt and ran when he raised a bushy black brow.

Brodie caught her easily by the waist and tickled her belly as she doubled over and squealed in mock protest. She wriggled against him, and the movement startled him when a familiar pounding began low in his belly. Often a result of close contact with *other* women. Never Kirsty. His muscles grew taut as his brain comprehended his body's reaction to his best friend.

When her elbow drove into his gut, his breath came out in an *oomph*, and he let go.

They faced one another, hands on their knees, and he blinked at the warmth that rushed through him. A smile curved her pink lips. His eyes travelled from her mouth to her neckline, her breasts rising and falling as she took in deep gulps of air.

He swallowed.

Something odd stirred inside Brodie as he tried to fathom what had changed. Her eyes still reminded him of a dark cup of coffee. Her thick, cherry waves fell across her shoulders; threads of deep red tipped with gold glistened and shimmered as her body dragged in another breath. He reached out and slid a silky strand between his fingers. Her plump lips were parted, and he bent forward to ki—

Kirstine froze, her eyes wide.

He dropped the lock of hair. Their gazes locked. "For the love of saints," he whispered. "When did ye become so lovely?"

Then the pony let out a whinny. She ducked her head and ran under his arm to collect the horse. Brodie followed behind her with the basket. Out of habit, he cupped his hands and squatted slightly to give her a leg onto the pony. A glimpse of her slender ankle and firm, stockinged calf sent a rush of heat through him.

"I need to talk to ye later." His hand rested behind her on the blanket; his fingers absently brushed the small of her back. "Lachlan and I met up at the Thistle Inn and had a conversation about the future."

She laid the basket on the crook of her arm and clucked to the horse. "Ye ken where to find me. I'll be waiting as always," she called over her shoulder.

Brodie watched her ride away. *What the devil just happened?* He'd been gone less than two months, and suddenly his fiddle had decided Kirsty was an attractive female. Of course, she was, but... he scowled at her retreating figure. He hadn't eaten much. Maybe he was just lightheaded.

"Aye, that's it. I need sustenance," he declared to his horse as he mounted. Without another thought to the incident, he sent the gelding into an easy canter.

HE PAUSED AT the bottom of the lane and let out a satisfied sigh. *Home.* The aging castle, with its ancient round tower and square addition, had belonged to the MacNaughtons for centuries. The drafty medieval structure would continue to be the seat of their clan for generations to come—if his grandfather Calum had anything to say about it. And the man always had *something* to say.

A Scottish deerhound loped up from the stable. With a howl, it announced Brodie's arrival. His grandparents emerged from the castle, Calum in his traditional belted plaid, squinting down at him, and Peigi wrapped in a shawl, waving enthusiastically. Black Angus's long shaggy tail wagged a welcome as he took his place next to his master on the cobblestone. Calum dropped a hand to scratch the wiry, dark-gray coat.

"I didna expect to see ye until next week." His grandfather's broad chest expanded as he yelled, "I hope it's no' bad news."

Brodie shook his head. A young stable lad with red curls came ran up to take his horse. "Ye'll be pleased, Grandda." Dismounting, he tossed the rein to the boy and ambled to his grandmother for a hug. "Miss me?"

Peigi nodded and poked at the faded red curls that had escaped her kertch. "Like I'd miss fresh butter on a warm biscuit." Her green eyes slanted as she took him in. "Ye need a good meal. Ye've lost weight."

Calum laughed. "The lad's been home but a moment, and ye want to feed him already."

"It's better than whisky on an empty belly." She wagged a finger at her giant of a husband. "No drinking until he's eaten something. It's barely afternoon, and I'd wager he missed breakfast."

Brodie gave her a loud kiss on each cheek and turned to his grandfather, arms held out, wiggling his brows. "Grandda?"

"Dinna even consider it, lad." But he wrapped his arms around Brodie anyway and thumped him on the back.

He was considered a younger, shorter version of his grandfather.

Now, Brodie noticed a bit more gray in the older man's black hair, a few more creases on his face and neck, but those deep blue eyes never faded. In fact, they studied him keenly. "We'll talk while ye fill yer belly, then we'll have a wee swallow and welcome ye home properly."

The threesome entered the castle, and the aroma of dried sage and fresh bread tickled his nose. His stomach rumbled again. To the right was a huge receiving room, still retaining the same ambiance it had before the Risings. The stone walls were covered in tapestries and banners of the MacNaughtons and those clans who pledged fealty to them. A huge fireplace took up half of one wall and large carpets scattered the floor. The stories above held a dining room and great hall for entertaining.

To the left was the tower. It held the family's private quarters. They climbed the narrow, dim stairway and entered the smaller family dining area. Here, the décor changed to quiet elegance and comfort. The walls were polished panels of light oak, and a long walnut table with intricately carved chairs took up the center of the room. Over the stone and marble hearth, his great-grandfather and faithful deerhound glowered at them from a heavy gilded frame. Brodie had hated that portrait as a boy; those sapphire blue eyes seemed to follow him about the room.

Cheese and breads were already set out. Calum poured them both some ale and pushed the plate of cold meat toward his grandson. "The cheese is especially good," he commented as Brodie scooped butter onto a scone.

"I'll try that next," he said around a mouthful. "I've only had a couple stale oatcakes since early this morning." He took a pull of the ale and smacked his lips. "Where's Ma?"

"With yer sister and an injured sheep. Brigid saw it limping and insisted the leg needed to be wrapped," his grandmother informed him. "Yer brother, Lachlan, is gone, so Glynnis said she'd assist."

"That lass does love her beasties. If it's no' a sheep, it's a calf or foal or some wild creature." Brodie shook his head. "They bring out her gentler side."

"If she showed half as much compassion to her suitors—"

"Dinna start, Calum," said Peigi. "She's young and in no hurry. Leave her be."

"Weel, I see nothing has changed in my absence." Brodie chuckled. "Grandda's right, though. She'll never attract a husband when she has to prove she can outride and outhunt the poor mon."

"Exactly my point," agreed Calum. "A male wants a woman who's soft and pliant, not trying to beat him in an arm-wrestling match."

"Is that what ye called me when we met? Soft and pliant?" asked Peigi, her tone deceivingly light.

"Och, woman, ye willna lead me into that trap." Calum bent over and placed a noisy kiss on his wife's mouth. "Ye stole my heart from the first. It didna matter if ye were pliant, only willing."

She smacked his chest but gave him a pleased smile before she turned back to her grandson. "The bonfire for Beltane will be held in Dunderave. Ye've arrived just in time."

Brodie rubbed his hands together. Good food, whisky, and lasses in their best gowns wanting to dance. The Edinburgh girls were bonny enough, but his heart belonged to the Highland pretties. The first of May was always a braw celebration.

"Ye'll behave yerself, lad," warned Calum. "Ye're two and twenty and need to look for a wife, no' sample the brew."

He rolled his eyes but said nothing, not in the mood for another lecture. "I saw Kirstine down by the Dunderave path. Her pony had thrown her."

"No! Is she all right? Shall I go by and check on her?" asked Peigi. His family had always liked Kirsty.

He shook his head but glanced at his grandfather, who now had a familiar glint in his eyes. "Only her pride wounded."

"Now there's a fine lass if ye want my opinion," Calum said.

"Comes from a good family, her da works hard tending the cattle and sheep, and her ma is a healer."

Brodie snorted. "Sounds like a list of wifely qualities. We're close but no' in that way. I've had this conversation with Ma." He popped a slice of meat into his mouth and chewed in silence. His mind strayed to the earlier encounter with Kirsty and his body's reaction to her. A natural consequence from such close contact. He'd have to be careful of that in the future. They weren't children any longer, as his ma had often reminded him.

"I saw Lachlan at the Thistle. On his way to Glasgow." Brodie hoped to turn the conversation.

"Aye, yer brother needed a wee respite from Ross Craigg and the bickering. His temper gets the better of him."

"Lachlan would rather give him a skelping than a lecture," he agreed. "Craigg's a blethering *eejit* who beats his women but avoids a mon's fist."

"Aye, and I wouldna trust him if he swore on his mother's grave." Calum scratched his jaw. "But now I have two grandsons gone."

"By the by, Lachlan and I discussed the mill and may have found a solution to our problem."

The MacNaughtons were partners in a textile mill in Glasgow. Brodie's aunt had married a wealthy Englishman who had financed the venture but left the daily operations to his in-laws. It seemed English earls could invest in trade, but not dirty their hands with it. Calum had accepted his son-in-law's proposition and put the entire clan to work, either at the factory itself, providing the raw wool, or weaving special order tartans.

Lord Stanfeld refused to travel to the Highlands, but he agreed to bring his Scottish wife to Glasgow several times a year for a family visit and to discuss business. Once their son, Gideon, was born, the two families had taken an annual summer trip to the town so the Mac-Naughton cousins would know their English kin. Since the old earl's death, their cousin Gideon had assumed the earldom, and Ian had taken over the business trips for Calum.

"Ian's no' been successful finding a replacement for the supervisor. He hadn't thought his absence would be extended like this, especially with a new wife." Brodie busied himself with a piece of bread and another slice of meat but kept a side eye on his grandfather. "We hoped, perhaps, Ian could come home for a while. Let Lachlan stay in Glasgow. I can accompany you when needed for the chief's duties."

Calum scowled, his thick brows pulled together. Peigi laid a hand on his arm. "Ye willna be getting any grandchildren from a couple who are separated."

"*Hmmph!* I suppose that's true enough."

"Weel, that's settled then." Brodie moved swiftly to the next subject. "And I'm happy to announce that we have signed a thirty-year lease on the building along the Water of Leith. By next year, we'll have another mill in Edinburgh."

"And after thirty years?"

"First option to buy or lease for another thirty."

"Saints and sinners!" bellowed Calum. "Excellent work, lad. Excellent work. Time for the good scotch." He peeked at his wife, who rose with a sigh.

"I'll leave ye both to yer whisky," she said as she moved toward the door. "Dinna overdo it. Ye'll have plenty of time to drink with yer grandsons at the end of the week."

"Just a wee swallow, *mo chridhe*," Calum said with a wink. "Just a wee swallow while we finish talking business."

BRODIE STRODE OVER the sandy hill, between the shrubs of yellow gorse, the chain on his sporran a soft *chink* to the rhythm of his stride. He'd wanted to walk, take in the smells, the sights, the sounds he'd missed the past month and a half. New grass scented the air and cushioned his step. Spring flowers in late bloom danced at his feet. A hawk soared overhead, spotted a chattering rodent, and dove for its supper. He enjoyed travel—new places, meeting people—but this was his home. His foundation. Space. After a week away, he longed for the rugged mountains dotted with pine and the pastures of bleating sheep and ambling cows.

He thought of relatives and ancient Scottish surnames that had been forced to relocate. There would never be anything as beautiful as this country. But so many families had been cast out in the past decades. Large landowners had eliminated the small farmers, turning their property into sizeable blocks for grazing cattle, then sheep. Leases weren't renewed, rents were raised, or only cash accepted. The clans had shrunk in size as people were forced out of homes occupied for centuries. Some had relocated to the coast as crofters and fishermen or emigrated to Canada or America. If his Aunt Maeve hadn't married a rich Englishman, the MacNaughtons might have endured the same hardships. Instead, their clan thrived, along with any smaller clans that had joined with them, including Kirsty's family, the MacDunns.

He made his way back to the path and around the bend, where a cluster of buildings came into view. His gray deerhound lumbered up to him, its long, shaggy tail wagging lazily. Brodie bent to scratch behind the dog's ears and suffered several wet licks. The hound had been a gift from his grandfather a couple of years ago, but it preferred Kirstine's company. She had taken care of the dog when Brodie had travelled to Glasgow last year, and he'd never been able to lure it back.

"How ye doing, Charlie?" The dog howled and thumped its tail in response. "I'd rather wake up to her face than mine too. Can't blame ye."

He entered the small courtyard and scanned the property. The cottage was about a hundred years old, with a thatched roof and limewashed stone walls. The old blackhouse, a long double-walled structure built of flat rocks, held the livestock. Several other, smaller stone buildings were scattered behind the house.

With a crack of his knuckles, he knocked on the heavy planks.

"Weel, if it isna Brodie MacNaughton." Mrs. MacDunn, a plump woman of average height hailed him from the open window with a tight smile. The shutter slammed shut, and she met him at the door. A white kertch covered her flour streaked, dark brown hair. She adjusted the worn brown shawl pulled over her striped green and tan gown.

"Kirstine, ye have a visitor," she called to her daughter, wiping wet dough from her hands on her apron. "So, ye've returned home, I see."

Her tone was polite but lacked warmth. Brodie got along well with Mr. MacDunn, but something had changed Mrs. MacDunn's attitude toward him several years ago. Around the time Kirstine turned seventeen. It wasn't his fault that her daughter had turned down two suitors. Sure, Kirsty had asked his opinion. Sure, he had made it known that neither man was good enough for her. But she'd been a grown woman of eighteen, then nineteen, and made up her own mind.

Kirstine peeked over the loft, then scrambled down the ladder, her skirt in one hand. "I'll be back in an hour or so, Ma." She grabbed Brodie's hand and pulled him back outside. "She's in a foul mood today. We're best away from the cottage."

As Kirsty pulled him along, that strange stirring in his belly returned. He tried to quell it, recognized it as the early signs of a new romantic involvement. This was his best friend. And he needed her. If they went down that path together, he might lose one of the people most important to him. Women seemed to come and go in his life, but Kirsty was his constant support, his rock.

She threaded her fingers through his as they ambled down the lane. The touch of her skin sent a warm jolt through him... excitement and disquiet at the same time. Not a good combination.

CHAPTER TWO
Altering Aspirations

MERCIFUL HEAVENS! HOW she had missed him. Earlier that day when he'd pulled her from the ground, Kirstine had wanted to throw her arms around his neck and kiss him full on the mouth. She hadn't, of course. Yet... Brodie had turned a spill from a pony into a moment of passion. The first between them.

Kirstine had recognized the moment he'd realized it, sensed the shock when he reached out and fingered her hair. His touch made her skin dance. She'd held her breath, her insides quaking, as new sensations rippled through her body. Then the eejit pony had snorted, and the hunger in Brodie's dark blue eyes faded. So, she'd ran to calm her own pounding heart.

"What did ye want to talk about?" She settled into their usual comfortable pace with fingers entwined and arms swinging between them. "It sounds important."

Kirstine wore a champagne walking dress with apricot trim and a sash that she'd sewn herself. An old London fashion magazine, *La Belle Assemblée*, had been passed around between the local girls. Though the sketch had been several seasons old, it was still much better than the outdated clothes the villagers wore. Her free hand fingered the apricot lace scallops along the collar. Her mother had scoffed at the high waist and lower neckline, declaring the English fashions had no place for working folks. Good sturdy clothes were fine enough unless there was a service or a cèilidh. There hadn't been a sizeable gathering since Hogmanay, and those New Year festivities had been months ago. Kirstine was ready for some amusement.

"I stopped at the Thistle on my way home from Edinburgh," he began, swinging her arm back then forward, "and ran into Lachlan on his way to Glasgow."

"That's for the best. Ross Craigg has been muttering to anyone who will listen since his dispute with my uncle over some sheep. Craigg paid for some lambies, but disease swept through last month, and half of them died. Uncle tried to pay Craigg back, but the mon wanted a prize ewe instead of the coin." She smirked. "Your grandfather accepted my uncle's cash and gave Craigg some MacNaughton lambs. Now Craigg tells everyone that Lachlan threatened his hide if he didna accept the terms offered by the MacNaughton."

"That mon could argue with a mute. I'd wager he was found in the woods and adopted into that clan. It's beyond comprehension that he comes from the same blood as Lissie." Brodie pulled her off the path and over to a clearing. They had a view of the mountains in front of them, a jagged skyline of brown and greens capped with white. "Lissie and Ian have a part in what I want to talk about."

He unclasped his plaid and spread it on the ground. Kirstine sat down and hugged her knees. Brodie stretched out next to her, propped on his elbow, his head in his palm. Her gaze trailed down his body from the linen shirt open at the neck, down the muscular thighs, to the thick calves. He was a fine-looking man who, she realized, was oddly quiet.

His fingers traced the bold lines on the plaid, his eyes narrowed in concentration. Kirstine wanted to push that thick, black curl from his forehead and comfort him. She sensed the urgency in his silence.

"Come out with it," she urged quietly. Her chin rested on her knees, but she turned her head to keep an eye on him. "Ye always feel better when ye think out loud."

"Aye, if I'm with ye when I do it. Others just try to tell me how they would solve the problem." He sighed. "My brother, Lachlan, doesna feel he is the right choice for chief when Grandda steps down. He's of the opinion I would be a better candidate."

She nodded and waited.

"He has no patience and hates to placate grown men who bicker with one another. I argued against it. He was no' considering of the serious issues the chief deals with and the leadership the MacNaughton provides." Brodie sat up, both arms behind him now, his head thrown back. "Grandda willna like it."

"What are yer feelings? Would ye welcome the responsibility?"

He was silent for a long while. "Aye, I believe I would. I have the temperament to deal with people fairly."

"So do I," she said simply. Brodie needed to come to his own conclusions.

"How do I convince Grandda? Lachlan has tried to talk to him, and he willna listen. Says he just needs more time to learn the ways of negotiation." Brodie chuckled. "Lachlan has a knack for *trade* negotiations, not diplomacy. I've never seen a mon enjoy haggling more than my brother. He's the MacNaughton that should run the mill. Ian should be home with his wife."

"Haggling and negotiating are different things, and yer grandfather kens it. He'll come around."

"Ye think so?"

"Aye, ye're clever at solving problems, always have been. Ye can be impartial, and everyone likes ye." Kirstine leaned back on her elbows, side by side with him now, their faces turned up to the sky. Fluffy bits of white hung in the pale blue, rearranged into vague shapes, and floated away. The sunshine warmed her skin, and a soft breeze flipped up the hem of her skirt. "What does this have to do with Ian and Lissie?"

"Ye ken the supervisor at the mill quit. Ian must stay until a replacement is found, and that has no' been going well. Lachlan wants to share the duties in Glasgow. Give Ian more time to spend here with Lissie and start his family."

"And?"

"Grandda has agreed to that much for now. Lachlan expects me to persuade the MacNaughton to let him stay at the mill. I'm afraid I'd have to enlist the help of the faeries to work that kind of magic."

She chewed her bottom lip. "Instead of telling yer grandfather, ye need to show him. Go with him as Lachlan did, but speak up so he not only hears yer ideas but sees other men's reactions. That will convince him quicker than words."

He nodded. "Aye, there have been several instances I might have approached a dispute differently. Och, it wasna worth the argument at the time but now..."

She rested her cheek against her knees and smiled at him. "Now, you want yer voice heard."

Brodie leaned over and whispered in her ear, "I love ye, lass. I kent ye would help me through this."

"By listening? Anyone can do that." She laughed, his nearness warming her skin. "Ye always have the answers in yer head, Brodie. Ye just need to dig around all the uncertainties and find what's in yer heart."

"Ye're my neutral territory. I dinna have to choose my words so carefully with ye. With others—even my family—I must worry over whose feelings I might hurt or whose temper might flare if I dinna express myself well. I canna just spout off ideas to solve a problem, in case my intent is misinterpreted."

His consideration of others was one reason she loved him so. Sure, he had his faults, acted like a green lad when it came to his female infatuations, but he would see his folly in that respect. Brodie would be a confident and honorable chief who would serve his clan well.

He sat up, and the pressure of his shoulder against hers sent her pulse racing. He turned his head, his breath hot against her neck.

"Will ye always be here for me, Kirsty? Ye're like family." He took her hand in his. His thumb stroked her skin, and a swell of pleasure coursed through her belly. "There has always been something special between us."

Merciful heavens! This was it. She held her breath; her heart pounded so hard she was certain Brodie could hear it. He bent his head. She closed her eyes.

And then he kissed her on the cheek and stood, tugging her to her feet. "I should get ye back before yer ma takes a skelp at my noggin."

Her face flushed at the images that flooded her brain. The *thump* slowed along with the disappointment. She blinked quickly at the sudden burn in her eyes.

Patience! He's coming to his senses, her heart whispered.

Slap him! her brain urged as she suppressed a giggle.

They walked back down the lane, and he asked what she had done during his absence.

"Well, the Widow Weir fell, trying to hitch her own wagon and bumped her head. Her horse—"

"Och, but I saw some pretty ponies in the city. One was a fine bay, wasted as a carriage horse just standing around waiting for a customer. I saw it as I left a fine establishment my first night there." The rest of their exchange revolved around his time in Edinburgh. Conversations usually spun back to Brodie. Kirstine didn't mind; she enjoyed the deep timbre of his voice.

His blue eyes twinkled with humor when he described a comical tavern scene that involved a stray mutt, a barmaid with a full tray, and a drunken patron. He soon disarmed her with his genuine smile, and she decided not to ponder their closeness and just enjoy the moment, this time alone with the man she loved. When he began to laugh, pulling her into his side, his arm lazily slung across her shoulders, the flutters in her stomach increased.

Someday, Kirsty told herself, *someday soon.* Her conviction had held strong all these years. After today, seeing the heat in his eyes, she couldn't give up. Deep inside her soul, she knew Brodie would be hers.

>>>><<<<

"AND WHAT WAS so important he couldna talk to ye here?" asked her mother, scouring the stained and dented wood next to the dry sink. With a sharp blade, she sliced a hunk of venison and added it to a pot simmering over the grate.

"Leave the lass alone," chided her father as he filled his pipe. He held a long, thin tinder toward the hearth's embers, set it to the carved wooden bowl, and puffed at the fragrant tobacco. "Brodie just returned, and they needed some privacy."

Her ma snorted. "For what? Advice? If they truly needed privacy, I'd give them the cottage and go outside myself. The lad is no' likely to settle on a wife for some years to come. And my only daughter is getting older." She tossed a scrap to Charlie. The *chomp* of his jaws made them all smile as he caught the piece of gristly meat midair.

"There's nothing wrong with a young man seeing what he has to choose from. When he comes to us for Kirstine's hand, he'll ken he's got the best woman in these hills." Mr. MacDunn chewed on his pipe, his red and gray beard wiggling as his jaw worked. "That smells divine, *mo ghràdh.*"

"Yer sweet talk willna distract me." She wagged a finger at her husband, but the pink in her cheeks told him she was pleased.

"Ma, please. Could we talk later?" Regardless of the harsh tone, Kirstine knew her mother was only worried she'd be hurt. "What shall we bring for Beltane?"

Mrs. MacDunn recited the full menu—to her present knowledge—

provided by the villagers. Mr. MacDunn grunted occasionally, his hazel eyes following Kirstine as she swept the floor near the fire. She turned her back against his scrutiny and busied herself washing the turnips and potatoes for soup.

"I stopped to check on the Widow Weir yesterday. The lump on her noggin is better. No more swelling, only a faded bruise." Kirstine grinned. "She's a survivor, that one."

Her mother laughed. "Aye, I hope to be as tough when I'm her age." She wiped her hands on her apron. "One of the villagers sent word they need more loosestrife tincture. Spring chills have given several of the children sore throats. A few good gargles should do the trick."

"That plant will be in bloom shortly. We're low, so I'll add it to my list and collect more." Kirstine prided herself on keeping their medicines stocked.

After dinner, her father went out to the blackhouse to feed the livestock.

"Now tell me what's happened. I saw a different kind of excitement in yer eyes when he came calling." Ma sat down at the table and brushed crumbs from the varnished surface onto her apron. "Did he kiss ye?"

Kirstine's cheeks flamed. "Och, no, but I thought he would. I told ye I fell from Speckles when I was gathering herbs, and he came upon me while I was flat on my backside. He helped me up and we... he tickled me, and before I knew it, we were both nose-to-nose, and his eyes had turned a stormy blue."

"And that's no' happened before?"

She shook her head. "He reached out for a strand of my hair, rubbing it between his fingers, and stared at it as if he'd never seen such a thing. Then Speckles whinnied, and I didna ken what to do, so I ran."

"Ye ran?" Her mother threw her hands in the air. "And this afternoon?"

"Nothing. Back to the old Brodie."

Another familiar snort. "Weel, we need to pretty ye up for the cèilidh. Even if he doesna notice, there will be other fine young men in attendance."

"I dinna want—"

"Ye also dinna want to be alone, do ye? Yer twenty years old, my dear, and time is no' on yer side when it comes to marriage." She stood and cupped Kirstine's cheek with one palm. "If he hasna made his intentions clear by the end of the summer, ye need to put him behind ye."

The pesky tears burned her eyes again, but she blinked them back. "I canna marry another when my heart belongs to Brodie. How can ye ask that of me?"

"Then ye better let him ken how ye feel." Her mother grunted with disgust. "A nod is as good as a wink to a blind horse. Subtlety doesna work on mutton-headed men. I say, a little competition would be a good way to open his eyes."

⇒⟫⟪⟸

BRODIE PICKED UP speed and broke into a run, paying no attention to the bleating sheep that griped at him or the rhythmic *thump* of his sporran against his thighs. He needed to rid himself of this tension, the tightness in his chest and… other places. Sort out what had changed between Kirsty and him in such a short time.

He'd wanted to kiss her *again*. And what the hell had she been wearing? Where were her usual simple wool skirts and modest necklines? This afternoon he had seen the outline of her body through that thin gown. The beige muslin material, with light orange ribbons and embroidery, had cast a golden glow over her skin. The flimsy shawl had done nothing to cover her curves. When she'd leaned back, exposing her neck to the warm sunshine, he'd glimpsed the creamy swell of her bosom. His fingers had itched to trace the lace, slide under the delicate border, and stroke the soft fullness beneath.

A low growl worked up his throat. Was she trying to look like the proper misses that strutted about Glasgow and Edinburgh? She was a Highland lass, not a debutante.

The devil take him! Sweat dripped down his neck, under his shirt. A sweet ache penetrated his muscles the longer he ran; his lungs burned but it cleared his head. By the time he stopped at the swimming hole, he panted, hands on his knees, and sucked in great gulps of air. Then he peeled off his clothes and dove into the clear, cold water. He swam toward the waterfall and stood under it for a while. Let the falling drops pound the soreness from his shoulders and chest.

His muscles relaxed, and his natural optimism returned. He'd spent too many days in the saddle, that was all. The run had released that excess energy, the pent-up excitement from the business ventures and bustling city.

When he swam back to the rocky bank, he found his sister Brigid on the jumping boulder. She waved a cold meat pie at him, took a bite, and grinned. "Ye ken how many lasses would like to be where I am right now?"

He laughed. "Ye minx. Turn yer head so I can dry off."

"What's it worth to ye?"

"Does everything have to be a bargain with ye?" He sighed and ran both hands through his wet hair, smoothing it back. "What if I dinna whip yer hide when I catch ye?"

"Ye canna catch me." She stuck out her tongue. "But since I havena seen ye in so long, I'll do ye a favor."

"How grand of ye, sister." He grabbed his plaid and rubbed himself down quickly, yanking on his shirt. "I'm good."

Brigid turned back to him, her long auburn curls flashing in the late afternoon sun. She watched him in silence as he wrapped the kilt around his waist and secured it. He sat down to put his stockings back on, and she climbed down the rock to plop beside him.

"I'm starving, sweet sister. Can ye spare half of that?" His mouth watered as she took another bite of the flaky crust.

A bit of carrot missed her mouth and plopped onto her lap. With a wicked smile, she gave her other dirty hand an obligatory wipe against her skirt, picked up the gravy-covered chunk, and tipped her head back to drop it into her open mouth.

"I'm hungry too, dear brother." She took another bite and chewed slowly with her lids closed, groaning loud enough to set the hounds to howling. Her feet wiggled back and forth, the coarse brown skirt halfway up her calves, revealing her dirty stockings and muddy boots.

"Have ye been chasing piglets? Ye need a wash yerself, ye filthy lassie."

"At least I'm no' barefoot. Ma is happy I'm at least covering my toes." She leaned over and kissed him on the cheek. "I missed ye."

Brodie grinned. He and Brigid were the youngest and had always been close. His mother said he'd been the only one who could soothe his sister as an infant. He still had a knack for calming her temper, though it took more effort as she grew older.

"Do ye want to go hawking tomorrow? Enid's ready." Brigid referred to the bird she'd found injured and tended to over the winter. "We've no' gone since November."

"Ye named the hawk after our cook?" he asked as he crisscrossed and tied his laces. "What was the reasoning behind that?"

"They both have a ferocious scowl but are good at what they do."

Brodie howled with laughter. "I've missed ye, too, Brigid. And aye, we'll go tomorrow."

His sister's eyes narrowed. "We've been collecting wood for the bonfire. Mairi's asked about ye."

Mairi. A bonny redhead with freckles, a pert nose, and ample bosom. A perfect diversion. Perhaps she'd chase away these peculiar sensations.

Brigid wrinkled her nose when he grinned. "What about Kirsty? If ye had half a brain—"

"Which I dinna, as ye and Ma often remind me when it comes to her."

"She's a silly thing. I dinna ken how ye put up with such giggling lasses."

"The same way I put up with a domineering, nosy sister." He stood and helped her to her feet. "With copious amounts of patience, humor"—he leaned over and snatched the last bite of pie while pushing her into the water—"and swift feet!"

Brodie let out a guffaw as Brigid spluttered and flapped, sending a wet spray over his head. He grabbed his shirt and sprinted up the grassy slope. His sister's curses floated after him, most of which should never grace a lady's ears, let alone come out of her mouth.

CHAPTER THREE
Fire, Ire, and Passion

THE POUNDING OF a hundred hooves sounded against the earth. The crowd parted and the Highland cattle thundered past them. Brodie loved tradition. Tomorrow was Beltane. The celebration of the coming of summer. Tonight, May Eve, was his favorite of the activities. The Craiggs drove their fold past the bonfire, a blur of red and dun shaggy hides with pointed horns. Everyone cheered as the beasties settled into their summer pasture.

Next, those who fancied themselves brave enough or drunk enough would leap over the flames of the bonfires before they grew too high. A rainbow of orange, red, and yellow melted together as the sun set. Smaller fires were lit, and smoke curled upwards with the aroma of roasted meat. The clank of wooden and tin mugs blended with raucous laughter, the giggles of children, and their mothers' reprimands. Several men from smaller clans hurdled the growing blaze. One boy singed his backside, and his mother chased him around with a poultice. Brodie figured the lad's face was redder than his bum.

"Ye ken ye have to jump for our family with both Ian and Lachlan gone." Brigid poked him in the side, dark cherry waves brushing her waist. The MacNaughton blue eyes flashed with challenge. "I'd do it for ye, but I promised Ma to behave like a *lady* tonight."

"*Hmmph!* And perhaps Bossie the cow will fly over the moon." Brodie spotted Kirstine by the food table. Mairi was nearby, making eyes at him and smiling. His gaze drifted back to Kirstine, and suddenly Mairi lost some of her shine. Her hair was too frizzy, her freckles too numerous, her body too full. Where Kirstine seemed to be…

"Are ye all right? Ye have a queer look on yer face." Brigid popped the last bite of a tart into her mouth and sucked the crumbs off her thumb and forefinger. She followed his eyes. "Kirstine gets bonnier every year. It's a wonder she's no' married."

"It's no' my fault," he groused.

Brigid's eyebrows shot up. "No one said it was. Perhaps I'll introduce her to the widower, MacDougal, since ye're no' interested. He's got a young son, and they just came back from the coast."

He ignored her attempt to make him jealous. "Tried his hand at crofting?"

"Aye, but he couldna make a living at it. Worked in a fishery and hated it. Grandda hired him to help with the animal husbandry." Brigid wiped her fingers on her plaid and put her hands on her hips. "He's in charge of breeding an English stock with our sheep. MacDunn attempted it, but disease took the lambies."

"So I heard." His eyes remained on Kirstine.

"He's a handsome mon."

"MacDunn?"

Brigid elbowed him in the side. "Liam MacDougal, the widower. Do ye listen to anything I say? The tall one over there with the dark red hair, holding the lad's hand."

Brodie grinned. "May the heavens fall upon us. Brigid MacNaughton finds a mon attractive. Where is our mother? She'll fall on her knees in thanks."

"No' for me, ye eejit. For Kirstine. She's nigh on one and twenty. He's a wee old, in my opinion, but ye canna tell by his face." She pursed her lips. "And the child looks no more than five. Ye ken how Kirsty likes to cluck over the bairns."

He grunted. Why *did* Brigid playing matchmaker put a knot in his stomach? "Weel, I'm off to warm my backside. Wish me luck."

"Ye'll need it after waiting so long. The fire's building," she called after him.

"My grandson, Brodie, will be next to jump." Calum held up a hand. "I dinna ken if he waited for the fire to grow because he's so verra brave or if his arse is just cold."

As the crowd chuckled, Brodie sprinted and leapt over the fire, the spindly flames licking at the hairs on the back of his thighs. He landed in a crouch on the other side, stood, and raised his arms in victory.

"May the sun shine bright, our pastures remain green, our livestock healthy, and our children's children be raised upon this land." Calum held up a cup, met with shouts of approval.

The night sky turned a deep purple as the last of the daylight sank behind the mountains. The keening wail of a bagpipe took precedence, and the clan members bowed their heads for the first song of the evening. It was a Gaelic ballad of warriors and blood and courage. When the final notes faded, someone yelled, "Something a wee more jovial, if ye please!"

A fiddler dragged a bow across his strings, and several pipers joined to fill the night air with the twang and whistle of ancient musical instruments. Several men formed a line, the traditional dance steps light and quick as fine wool kilts rose and fell to the rhythm of the tune. Applause echoed as the song finished, and the men took a bow. A Scottish reel began. The dancers circled around the fire with their arms entwined. Onlookers clapped to the quick, boisterous beat as their clansmen completed the centuries-old ritual.

Brodie looked up at the stars, brilliant against the black sky. The first couples weaved past him, and he scanned the faces for Kirstine. His grandparents joined the dance, and he saw his mother lift her skirt as she caught a neighbor's hand to be pulled into the fray.

Fingers covered his eyes from behind, and he smiled. "I was looking for ye. Would ye to care dance the next reel?"

"I've been looking for ye too," whispered a voice in his ear. "I'd love to be yer partner."

Shite! It wasn't Kirstine. With reluctance, he turned to acknowledge Mairi's beaming face. *Come, ye dunderhead*, he scolded himself, *ye counted on this lass to distract ye.*

"Good evening, Mairi," he said with a bow. "Are ye enjoying yerself?"

"Aye, and more so now." Her green doe-eyes searched his face. "Ye were looking for me?" She took his hand and pulled him into the group of dancers lined up for the next set. "It must be yer lucky day, then."

It was a fast-paced dance, and he and Mairi were breathing hard by the end. "Shall I get ye something to drink?" he asked politely. Her freckles blended into her red cheeks as her fingers smoothed her frazzled curls.

"Aye, I'll wait for ye away from the fire." She nodded toward a long tree trunk laid out as a bench. It was shadowed by a small group of pines.

Brodie was pouring a sweet watered wine for Mairi and had just added a portion of whisky to his own when Kirstine approached.

"I see Mairi found ye," she said. "She certainly has the energy for a reel."

"And ye have the grace for it," he answered with a smile. "I was looking for ye when she surprised me from behind. I hoped it was ye."

"Every time I try to find ye, someone else stops me. Either a parent thanks me or Ma for help, or needs advice on a medicinal herb, or someone wants to dance." Kirstine accepted the cup he offered. "But I'm here now."

"And I must deliver this to Mairi." He thought disappointment darkened her eyes, but her lips turned up when he said, "Ye're lovely tonight."

Her flaming hair was pulled up with a ribbon, and her lustrous red waves spilled down her back. The bonfire highlighted the streaks of gold in the long curls and the flush of her cheeks. She wore another stylish, high-waisted gown that drew his gaze to her full breasts.

"That color blue looks bonny on ye." He wished he didn't have to bring any refreshment to Mairi. "Is it new?"

"Aye, I made it myself from a sketch I saw in a London fashion magazine. The color matched your eyes."

"So ye were thinking of my eyes when ye made it?" He wondered why that pleased him. "Or do ye say that all to the lads?"

"Ye ken I'm no' a flirt like that Brodie MacNaughton. He teases all the lasses and skips away just as they hand him their heart."

He leaned close, his nose brushing her cheek. "Perhaps one of them should chase me."

"Och, ye're too fast for me. Maybe Mairi could catch ye." She gave him a wink and sauntered away.

He scowled at her retreating back as heat washed over him. Was she playing the coquette? Where was his Kirstine, and who was this new woman he'd come home to? He walked back to Mairi. She reached for the mug and pulled him down beside her.

"Thank ye, Brodie," she gushed with a flutter of her lashes. "I'm parched."

Sparks shot out, one close to their feet, as a log collapsed into the embers. Orange flicked and trailed into the black night sky. The crackle and pop of charred wood added to the din of voices and boisterous singing. Long shadows pirouetted against the curtain of darkened woods, like a dark puppet show lit by the moon. When Mairi broke the silence to regale him with village news, he focused on the glowing flames and let his mind wander.

On the other side of the bonfire, he watched Kirstine. She smiled at the widower, her face turned up to him. He studied her profile and realized she had an adorable nose. The man returned her smile, and Brodie's stomach tensed. An unfamiliar feeling dropped in his chest, and his hand went there as if to wipe it away. But the little, tight ball grew.

"Are ye all right, Brodie? Do ye have a pain?" asked Mairi, concern in her eyes.

"Aye, er, I'm fine. Too much meat, I fear." He stood and held out his hand to help her to her feet. "I need to check on my grandfather. Thank ye for the dance."

⟫⟫⟫⟪⟪⟪

"I WANT YE to meet someone," Brigid said, pulling Kirstine by the hand. "His family was removed when the lords closed the open pastures for their sheep. He's back from the coast with his son."

Kirstine laughed but resisted. Brigid was a close friend and knew her feelings about Brodie. Perhaps she'd seen her brother with another and had the same idea about competition that her own mother had. "What are ye up to? Does he need help or are ye trying to marry me off?"

"Both," Brigid said with a grin. She waved at the tall, handsome man as he approached.

Liam MacDougal had dark red hair, light green eyes, and a sense of humor. As old as her mother, she guessed. When he smiled and asked her to dance, her reserve fell away. She liked him instantly. He was graceful for his height, and Kirstine enjoyed his company.

"I understand ye're knowledgeable with plants and herbs. Are ye one I could call when my son gets into mischief?" Liam escorted her away from the dancers as another tune began. He towered over her, but his demeanor was mild. "While I envy his energy, the lad isna the most graceful. He's already been stitched up more times than I have

31

myself."

"Aye, myself or my mother. We're always happy to help." Then he asked her what she enjoyed most about doctoring.

His expression of sincere interest soon had her chatting easily, and she shared the story of her first patient, a kid goat who'd cut himself on wire. She barely noticed he'd place a refreshment in her hand.

"So you stopped the bleeding, and it adopted ye?" He chuckled and refilled her cup.

"Its mother had died, so I became a surrogate." Kirstine tried to remember the last time she'd talked about herself at such length.

She turned the conversation back to Liam and his son, and their new home. As they sipped the cool wine, Brodie strolled up like a rooster and introduced himself.

"My sister says ye're working for us." He held out his hand. "I'm Brodie, the MacNaughton's youngest grandson."

"He's a good mon, yer grandfather. I appreciate the work," Mac-Dougal said. "He speaks highly of his grandsons."

Kirstine saw an unfamiliar gleam in Brodie's eyes. Almost surly, yet his tone was pleasant. "He's in the old cottage where ye were born, Brodie. Between the grazing pastures and the castle. Ye'll run into each other often, I suppose."

"I helped yer sister with an injured sheep the other day," MacDougal said. "She has a way with animals. I was impressed."

"If she had as much finesse with people—"

"I'm right behind ye, brother dear." Brigid punched Brodie in the shoulder, then turned to the taller man. "How do ye like my friend, Kirsty? I told ye she was a beauty."

Kirstine closed her eyes as heat flooded her cheeks. She could stomp on Brigid's foot right now. Brodie made an odd sound, something like a growl.

"We have several lovely widows"—he placed an arm over Kirstine's shoulders—"closer to yer age."

She gasped at his rudeness and pushed his arm away. "We're celebrating Beltane, not betrothals." Kirstine slapped at Brodie's hand as he tried to take hers. "Would ye like to dance again, Liam?"

A slow grin curved his lips. "I'd be honored, Miss MacDunn."

Kirstine bit back the giggle at the glare she knew was burning both their backs.

"I apologize for his remark," she said as the set began. "Brodie is usually most pleasant. I dinna ken what's got into him."

"Jealousy, if I wagered a guess."

I hope so, whispered the voice in her head. "We have no claim on one another, so it wasna proper for him to give ye that impression."

"I'm glad to hear it."

When the dance ended, MacDougal returned her to the refreshment table, and she introduced him to her mother. She endured more embarrassment while Ma gushed over the man and invited him for dinner. From the corner of her eye, she saw Mairi whispering to Brodie, his head dropped to listen. He gave the redhead that enigmatic MacNaughton smile—the one that could make any girl swoon—and her stomach dropped.

"He's just soothing his wounded pride," said Brigid. "Pretend ye dinna see."

This night had not gone as planned. Fantasies of her first kiss, clinging to his neck, Brodie's arms wrapped around her waist...

"Ye feckin' weasel! I'll kill ye if ye touch her again!"

The shout rumbled from wood behind Brodie, stunning those nearby into silence. Ross Craigg's stout form emerged from the trees, dragging Kirstine's cousin by the collar. Not another clash with Craigg! She gripped Brigid's hand.

"Da, it was only a kiss. Please, let him go," a fragile voice pleaded. "We're betrothed."

"Not with my permission," he raged. A strand of his thinning brown hair hung limp over forehead. His splotched face and bulbous nose contorted as the boy struggled beneath the tight grip.

Kirstine's uncle stormed across the field. "Let go of my son or I'll give ye a skelping ye'll no' survive," he bellowed, his red beard trembling, fists clenched. Her cousin tried to wrestle away from Craigg's grasp again but froze at his father's words. The girl sobbed and wrung her hands, her face tipped and hidden behind a veil of deep brown hair.

"He was groping my daughter, the piece of hog shite!"

"I asked her to marry me," the boy growled as he wiped blood from his nose. "Get yer stinking hands off me."

Kirstine held her breath as Craigg raised his other hand to smack her cousin, but her uncle caught the fist in mid-swing. The *crack* of bone hung in the air, and Craigg crumpled to the ground. Brodie rushed in to catch the unconscious man just before his head hit a rock.

"What the devil are ye thinking, mon?" demanded Calum, marching toward the group. "Ye're son is in the wood, alone with this lass, and ye punch her father? He'll want retribution for this." He made a motion to the fiddler, and the music began again.

"I lost my temper," muttered Kirstine's uncle. "He's had it coming."

"Aye, and I'm a wee jealous. Every mon in this glen has wanted to do that at one time or another," Calum admitted. "But he was within his rights this time, and he'll demand justice for the attack against him."

"Get something to revive the drunken cow. Quick!" Brodie propped the dead weight against his broad chest and fixed a stern scowl at the young couple. "And this incident is no' to be repeated."

Calum accepted a cup from a bystander and tossed it at the limp form.

Craigg spluttered and waved his arms in front of him. Kirstine saw Brodie wink at his grandfather.

"I canna hold ye back much longer, ye sodden hothead. Now

promise me ye'll no' hurt the lad for accidentally headbutting ye," Brodie said loud enough for anyone close to hear. "It's a holiday, and we'll settle it without violence."

Craigg blinked and rubbed his jaw. "What happened?"

Kirstine chewed her bottom lip. Would the ruse work? Brodie was clever, and she saw the spark of approval in the MacNaughton's eyes as he took the lead.

"Dinna play with me, Craigg, and no more whisky for ye tonight." Calum pointed to the boy, who still held a hand up to his face to staunch the blood. "I'll let the smashed nose pass, but no more fists. They're just young and got carried away."

Craigg scratched his chin and grimaced. "But what about my jaw?"

"What about it? I believe the boy might have given ye a Glasgow kiss in his exuberance to get away." Calum spread his hands, palm up, and shrugged his shoulders. "Unfortunate, but if ye didna drink so much, ye'd ken what happened."

"I thought—"

"Did ye see anything indecent besides a wee kiss," prodded Calum.

"No, but—"

"Weel, then it's just a matter of two disobedient children. Nothing we'll be needing a shotgun for." The MacNaughton smiled, and Kirstine saw where Brodie got every bit of his charm. "How old are ye, lad?"

"I'll be eighteen by Samhain," he mumbled from beneath his hand.

"And the lass?"

"She's sixteen," spit out Craigg. "I'd put a shotgun to my own head before I'd be joined to a MacDunn by marriage."

Brodie let the man go. "I dinna think such tragedy will be necessary. I've been caught in the woods a time or two myself without any harm done." He slapped Craigg on the shoulder. "Tell me ye've no' forgotten what it's like to be young?"

Craigg squinted at Brodie then shook his head as if to clear it.

"We're going home," he grumbled and took his daughter roughly by the elbow. She covered her face in her hands and continued to weep as he pulled her away.

No one liked Ross Craigg. Any witnesses were happy to see him get back what he often gave his wife and daughter. They also knew the girl would pay once the wagon was out of sight.

"That man will get his someday," Brigid said to Kirstine. "Fate has a way of giving ye back what ye've given most to others."

A chill slithered down Kirstine's spine. "I hope his wife and daughter survive to see it happen."

CHAPTER FOUR
Pleas and Promises

Ross snapped the reins, and the wagon lurched forward. His jaw ached from grinding his back teeth. A thorn in his side, those MacNaughtons. When Calum had married Peigi Craigg, the two clans had forged a peace, ending a decades-old feud. Then the Craiggs had pledged fealty to the MacNaughton, followed with years of tirades by Ross's father. Rants about the partiality toward Peigi's branch of the Craiggs over his own family, the favors given to them, the rewards handed out to *their* sons. The only comfort Da found was in the whisky that eventually claimed him. Even on his deathbed, his last words to his son had been to continue the enmity.

Dinna follow them like the rest of the bleatin' sheep. Keep yer own counsel and bide yer time.

They'd been left destitute. Without any income, he'd been forced to crawl to the man responsible for his father's death. His jaw clamped again at the memory. Calum had been reluctant to hire him at the mill, citing his family's penchant for drink. As if the MacNaughton wasn't known for his own "wee swallows" throughout the day.

Ross's mother had gone to Peigi, begged and pleaded for a job for her son. She had two more young ones and a bairn to feed. So, Ross had gone to Glasgow and worked the power looms twelve hours a day in a sweltering stone prison. Day after day after day. Who could blame a man for a few nips to pass the time? But some lass had gone blethering to the manager. He'd received a proper *laldie* for his misconduct and been sent to the docks. Heavy lifting and sweeping. A Craigg swishing a broom while a woman operated his machine. He brought a bottle every day after that. Until he accidentally knocked that young boy into the river.

It wasn't his fault the lad couldn't swim. Ross had tried to pull him out, but the boy wouldn't stop screaming. He'd only held his head under for a moment. To get the lad to be quiet, but he'd grown too quiet. The manager, a blustery Sassenach, had suspected foul play but couldn't prove anything. Still, Ross had been sent home in disgrace. That was when he'd found out how much his mother had changed. She refused him hospitality *in his own home*. And Calum had supported her, even sent one of his human sheep to guard the house.

Ross had vowed to get his revenge against the MacNaughtons. He'd followed his father's advice ever since: bided his time and kept his eyes peeled for small victories along the way.

Nessie sniffled beside him.

"Shut yer sniveling mouth!" He backhanded her to reinforce his request.

She'd caused enough trouble. Oh, how he'd wanted to plant a facer on that younger grandson tonight. It would be almost as good as smashing Lachlan's smug face. But Ross had been on the other end of a fist before, and it hurt like hell. He touched the bridge of his nose gingerly, then cringed at the pain in his cheek.

Being chief didn't give Calum the right to intervene in a man's business. And that whiny MacDunn. He'd been added to Ross's list.

"Ye're lucky I didna kill the feckin' eejit." He looked at his pathetic daughter, crying silently into her hands. "Tell me the truth. Did he touch ye? Under yer clothes? By devil's own hand, if he tried to put his—"

"No!" Nessie cried, the moon glinting off her wet cheeks as her hands fell away. She clutched at the bench for balance as the wheels hit a deep rut.

Her brown eyes, so like his own, blazed with hatred. For a moment, he thought she would strike him. Her own father. The ungrateful whore. "Go ahead." He nodded at her trembling fist and white knuckles.

Nessie's anger flickered and died. Her shoulders slumped, and she sucked in the growing sob. "N-nothing untoward happened, Da. It was only a kiss. I swear."

Ross reached over and threaded his fingers into her dark hair. Then he closed his fist and snapped her head back. "If ye ever go against me again, I'll squeeze yer scrawny neck until yer face turns blue and yer eyes pop out. Do ye understand?"

Nessie pressed her lids shut and nodded. A tear leaked out of one corner. "I promise to be good, Da. Just dinna hurt Hamish, please. I beg ye, dinna hurt him."

"Lovely. But ye ken it's my duty as a conscientious parent to discipline a willful and disobedient child. The high and mighty MacNaughton may stop in for a visit to be certain I didna abuse ye." He put the reins between his teeth and talked around the leather. "So, I must be careful when I administer my punishment."

He grinned for the first time in hours at the fear widening her eyes. "Aye, right. Ye understand it's yer own doing."

Ross pulled back his free arm and drove his fist into her stomach. She clutched her belly to curl around the pain as she gasped for air. He clucked sympathetically as he held her head back; her blinking eyes stared blindly toward the moon. Then he kissed her on the forehead and released his grip. "There, now we both feel better."

CHAPTER FIVE
Candor and Kisses

THE FIRST DAY of May dawned bright and clear. As she did every year, Kirstine ran to the nearest meadow at sunrise. Legend decreed if a lass washed her face with the morning dew on Beltane morning, her beauty would last longer. Brodie was waiting for her with his annual posy of wildflowers.

"Ye dinna need to scrub yer face." He handed her the bouquet. "Ye're bonny enough as ye are."

His raven hair clung to his square jaw and curled at his neck, as if he'd quickly washed his face and hadn't bothered to dry his skin. Her gaze hung on his mouth, turned up in a smile, showing straight white teeth. Her breath quickened, his flirtation with Mairi the previous night forgotten.

"Do ye no' like the flowers?" he asked. His boot shuffled the soft ground, sending wisps of morning mist spiraling around his ankles. "I picked them in a hurry because I didna want to miss ye. It's our custom, ye ken."

Kirstine nodded and chewed her bottom lip. Should she tell him how she felt before the Maypole festivities? The way he said "our custom" in that silky, deep voice made her belly quiver. No, she'd wait until tonight when she was dressed in a lovely gown with her hair twisted and tied with ribbons.

"I thank ye, kind sir." Kirstine giggled, taking the bouquet. "If the dew truly worked, I imagine even the vain men would try it."

"Perhaps they do." He stepped forward and held out a corner of his plaid. "Ye missed a spot." He dabbed at her jaw, drying her skin.

Her breath caught as his movement slowed. Looking up at him, she was trapped in that intense blue gaze. His thumb slid over her bottom lip and sent a thousand wings beating in her stomach.

"Ye dinna need to scrub yer face," he repeated.

Kirstine shook her head, eyes closed, and his forehead touched hers. Fire. His skin was like a hot flame licking at hers. *Kiss me!* Her heart screamed. *Merciful heavens, kiss me.* His mouth was so close; his breath fanned her chin. The scent of honey drifted between them, and she resisted the urge to lick her lips.

Aarroooo! They both blinked at the deep howl. Charlie came loping across the meadow and jumped against Brodie's arm.

Brodie grunted, scratched the dog's head, and pushed it to the ground. "And good morning to ye too, Charlie." He sighed and looped her hand into the crook of his arm. "I suppose we shall both escort ye home now."

Had she glimpsed disappointment in his eyes? She smiled as they strolled in a comfortable silence. The sun peeked over the mountains. The promise of a lovely day. Pinks and reds lit up the sky, a spectacular backdrop for the birds' morning song. Her bare feet were cold against the wet grass, and the smell of pine and earth and Brodie filled her nose.

"Do ye have an opinion of how I handled the Craigg catastrophe?" he asked.

She laughed. "I was proud of ye, Brodie, and so was yer grandda. I saw it in his eyes."

"Ye gave me good advice. Show him rather than tell him what I'm capable of." He tapped his forehead. "I'm a quick learner."

"Do ye think Craigg will let it lie?"

"He was too foxed to question it last night, but he'll figure it out, eventually. No' that anyone will admit to seeing MacDunn hit him."

"Ma's afraid he took his anger out on the poor girl after they left. She wants to check on her but is afraid she'll make it worse with a visit." Kirstine sighed. "The mon has a vicious temper."

"I doubt he lets her out of the house for weeks."

"My cousin fancies himself in love with her. He's stubborn. I dinna suppose he'll give up."

Brodie chuckled. "What does a tender young lad ken of love?"

"And what does the wise old Brodie ken of it?" She peeked at him from beneath her lashes. His linen shirt stretched across his chest, and the muscles of his arm bunched and tensed with each step. Everything about the man was so… masculine.

"No' a blasted thing, to be truthful."

"Ye've considered yerself in love enough times," she reminded him with a smirk.

"My point, exactly." They came to the edge of her property. "Ye're the one constant woman in my life that's no' a relation."

And I've been waiting forever and a day, that little voice taunted.

"I'll see ye later, then?" he asked at her door.

"I've no' missed a May Day celebration that I can remember."

"It's a braw day for a celebration," declared her father. He helped his wife and daughter from the wagon. "I dinna believe there's a lovelier lass here than my wife."

Kirstine grinned when her mother's cheeks stained a pretty pink. She wanted this in her marriage. The lasting affection, a man who would still make her blush after twenty years. Yet, she couldn't see herself finding that with anyone but Brodie.

She wore the deep champagne gown with the apricot embellishments again. Her hair was swept up and twisted with ringlets that tickled the back of her neck. Her mother had threaded more apricot ribbon through the loose chignon and added small white buds around the crown like a halo. She wiggled her toes in soft leather shoes, remembering her bare feet—and Brodie—earlier that morning.

Liam MacDougal appeared, a smaller version of himself holding his hand. The boy's riot of red curls bounced against his round freckled face.

"May I say how bonny ye look today, Miss MacDunn?"

The boy pulled on his father's hand. "She's beeootiful, Da."

Kirstine smiled and squatted down, holding her hand out to the child. "Hello, I'm Kirstine. It's nice to meet ye."

He placed a hand at his stomach and gave her a choppy bow, his cap falling off in the process. "I'm Liam MacDougal, just like my da."

"Ye certainly are." Kirstine picked up the cap and dusted it off for him before greeting his father. "How are ye, Liam? Did ye meet my da last night?"

"I've no' had the pleasure." Her father shook hands with the widower. "I imagine the younger ones are already gathered at the May pole."

Kirstine found Brigid waiting for her. A long, spindly pine trunk lay on the ground, long colorful strips of material tied to the top. A dozen girls scooped up the ends as Brodie and Calum lifted the pole and carried it to the pre-destined hole, sinking it into the ground.

The unmarried women, dressed in their Sunday finest and flowers in their hair, arranged the strips around the pole and stood in a circle. The young bachelors stood between them in their tartan kilts, silk hose, and best sporrans slung over their hips. Each grasped a ribbon as the drums pounded a slow ancient beat upon the stretched leathers.

Calum approached with a female child, entered the circle, and lifted her high. She placed a wreath of flowers on top of the May pole, and the crowd cheered. The dancers moved in two concentric circles, the women ducking under the men to weave the multi-colored strips in a plait around the pole.

The shorter the ribbons, the lower the participants had to bend to avoid the oncoming dancers. Kirstine passed Brodie, ducked low beneath him, and felt his hand brush her backside. When she looked over her shoulder, he winked. When the strips were too short to continue, the drums increased the beat and a frenzy of twirling bodies finished wrapping the bottom of the pole.

Silence fell, except for the huff of the participants catching their breath. Then the MacNaughton let out a bellow, followed by shouts and screams of delight. Kirstine searched the throng for Brodie. He spotted her at the same time, waved, and made his way toward her. She saw Mairi block his path, then MacDougal stepped in her line of vision.

"Would ye care for some refreshment?" he asked, his green eyes narrowed against the sun. "And perhaps a dance later?"

She looked around his tall, lanky form and saw the back of Brodie and Mairi. "Aye to both," she answered with a smile. "Have ye seen my parents?"

"Yer mother convinced yer father to bring her by the booths. She's of a mind to buy some pretties," he said with a grin.

As he walked away, Kirstine wondered if she should tell the man her heart was taken. Or would MacDougal consider her forward for jumping to conclusions? But she recognized the look in his eyes. He was interested. If it weren't for Brodie, she might return his attentions. A handsome man, lean but strong, with an adorable little boy. Kirstine loved children and hoped for many of her own. Boys with midnight hair, girls with deep brown hair, and all with the same sapphire blue eyes of the MacNaughtons.

Brigid hurried by, leading a nanny goat. "I see ye already have the widower's attention. Either he'll win yer heart or convince my pigheaded brother to take a stand."

She opened her mouth to argue, but Brigid had disappeared into the crowd. Kirstine disliked the type of woman who played one man against another. She refused to do it and decided to be honest with the widower.

"Thank ye," she said, accepting the cup from MacDougal when he returned. "Where is Liam, the younger?"

MacDougal laughed and nodded over her head. "Over there with his new friends. The boy isna shy, to be sure."

Kirstine turned to watch a group of children playing football and saw Brodie scowl at them. Mairi stood next to him, chatting to Calum and Peigi. Kirstine stuck out her tongue at Brodie and saw the corner of his mouth twitch.

"So, tell me why Mr. MacNaughton has not claimed ye but insists on glaring at me?" MacDougal took a long pull of his ale. "Is it me in particular he doesna like, or he just prefers ye to have *no* male attention?"

She choked on her sweet wine, and MacDougal patted her on the back.

"Are ye all right, lass?"

With a nod, she sucked in a breath then laughed. "I didna expect the turn in conversation. But I can understand why'd ye ask."

He crossed his arms and sent a glare in return. "Two can play this game."

Kirstine giggled. "To be honest, we dinna have any claims on each other, but…" *But what?* she thought. *I've been waiting for over a decade for him to realize he loves me?*

"But he's a fool and no' worth yer time if he canna make a commitment." MacDougal stared over her head and grinned. "I've done it now."

Brodie disengaged himself from Mairi and stormed in their direction. She closed her eyes and sighed. What was wrong with the man?

It was uncharacteristic of him to be so churlish.

"Kirstine, may I speak with ye in private?" Brodie asked, his teeth clenched.

She looked up at MacDougal, who nodded.

"I need to check on my son. Dinna forget the dance ye promised me." He threw back the last of his ale and ambled away.

"What was in yer porridge this morning? Something bitter, I have no doubt." Her irritation disappeared when he gave her a remorseful look. "What's so important?"

"I…thought… weel, you…" He shrugged his shoulders.

"Ye just didna want MacDougal paying attention to me." She sighed and set her cup on a nearby trestle. "But ye're right, we need to talk. Let's find someplace quiet."

They strolled to the outskirts of the festivities. There were several clusters of low-hanging trees and bushes, and Brodie steered them toward one, his hand hovering at her lower back. The first notes of a fiddle floated on the breeze, and the clansmen's chatter became a low hum in the background. She could still see people, so they weren't exactly alone, in case her mother saw them. She leaned back against a tree; the rough wood scratched her back through the material of her gown and kept her mind focused.

"I'm sorry, Kirsty. I dinna ken what has gotten into me. I get this tight knot in my belly when I see ye with MacDougal." He studied his boots, a frown pulling his black brows together. "I want what's best for ye, and he's too old. I bet he's as old as my ma."

"Lots of women marry older men."

"There's no reason for ye to settle for an old man."

"I'd hardly call him that." She struggled to hold back the grin.

He was jealous.

She was ecstatic.

"Weel, ye should keep looking. He's no' the one for ye." His gruff tone sent her pulse racing.

He bent his head, and that thick lock fell over his brow again. She wanted to reach out and push it back. So she did. It was soft under her finger, his skin smooth and warm. He looked up, his cerulean gaze a combination of heat and bewilderment. *She* had caused it, and the idea made her giddy.

"No and no." She looped her finger into his belt and pulled him forward a step.

"What?"

She licked her lips. Her mouth had suddenly gone dry. "No, I shouldna keep looking. No, he's no' the one for me."

Brodie nodded, his gaze now on her mouth, one brow arched in question. She swallowed.

"The only one in my heart is ye, Brodie MacNaughton." Kirstine lifted a finger and traced the square jaw, ran it down his neck. Her heart hammered in her ears as loudly as the drums during the May dance.

"Me?" Confusion skittered across his face, and then he nodded in understanding. "As yer best friend."

She gave him another tug, and his weight set them both off-balance, pulling her forward. When her back settled against the tree, his hands planted against the trunk and framed her face.

"That and more," she whispered. Her eyes closed as her courage slipped, and her knees tried to buckle. The rough bark bit into the skin between her shoulder blades.

"Look at me, Kirsty," he said, his voice soft and placating. "I care for ye as much as I do my own sister. But ye're my best friend, it would be like kissing Brigid."

Her lids flew open. Frustration and anger replaced the hesitation. Was she not pretty enough? Not flirtatious enough? What did all those other females have that she didn't?

"Is that what ye're worried about?" She pushed away from the tree. Brodie stumbled backwards, and she grabbed a handful of his shirt in both fists. When she pulled him down to her and pressed her mouth to his, Brodie stilled. His lips were velvety soft, and Kirstine was sure this was what ecstasy felt like. A low growl sounded from deep in Brodie's throat, and his hands wrapped around her waist to pull her roughly against him. Lightning struck through her center. *Merciful heavens!* She'd kissed a boy or two, a chaste kiss from one of her rare suitors. There was nothing chaste about this encounter, nothing boyish in Brodie's embrace.

Kirstine drew back, her body trembling, and gazed up at him. His expression had lost all humor, a storm brewing in his blue eyes. Her stomach twisted a bit at her own brazenness, but she didn't regret her actions.

"See if Mairi can boil yer blood like that." She moved past him to make a dramatic exit and save a scrap of her dignity.

A hand grabbed her elbow, and he eased her back against the tree. She closed her lids to block him out, embarrassment heating her face. Now he would appease her, spare her feelings.

"What the devil just happened, Kirsty?" His voice was husky, and it sent her pulse racing again. "That was no' the reaction I had expected. Did ye feel it too?"

His hand cupped her cheek while his thumb stroked her skin. A shiver ran through her as it brushed over her mouth. She concentrated on her breathing, then opened her eyes. He studied her as if they'd just met, and he liked what he saw.

"Aye, I felt it. And it was nothing like kissing a brother."

"No," he agreed, "and ye're right."

His breath was warm against her face. She tried to calm the *thud* of her heart. "I am?"

"Mairi could never boil my blood like that." His gaze focused on her mouth again. "But let's make sure it wasna some chance spark the fairies flung at us for their amusement."

Both hands cupped her face now, and he bent again, claiming her mouth. The blood pounded in her head. Heat rushed through her, and the only sensation she knew was his lips on hers, his touch, the fire licking at her skin.

Her hands lifted to his neck; her fingers slid into the dark curls. *More, I need more,* her body pleaded. His lips moved across her cheek, nibbled her ear lobe.

"By the saints, ye taste divine," he whispered. "I dinna understand what has happened between us, but I canna deny this stirring inside me. It's as if ye've bewitched me." He pulled back and held her gaze. "How long have ye kent?"

"Forever." The word had slipped out before she could stop it.

"Like a woman loves a mon?" he rasped in her ear, his warm breath fanning her cheek. "Are ye sure?"

Again, she nodded. "I ken my heart, Brodie." She shivered as his lips grazed the sensitive spot just below her ear.

"I need time to understand these new feelings, but I canna imagine life without ye, Kirsty. So let's see what happens." He closed her eyes with his mouth, and she breathed in his virile scent. Leather and soap and pine.

"There is no' a mon to compare with ye, in my opinion." A tempest brewed inside her. "I'll give ye time, but I canna wait forever."

He pulled her from the tree and held her close, his mouth creating a fiery path down her neck. "I *was* jealous, I expect. It's an odd sensation, and I dinna like it."

Kirstine pressed her body closer, an ache between her legs that she instinctively knew he could ease. His hardness pushed against her skirt, and he moaned. The sound, the power from that whisper of a groan, thrummed inside her and made her bold. Her hands traced the hard muscles of his neck, his shoulders. To finally tell him, to be able to touch him in this way filled her such sweet pleasure and... need.

"We should get back," he mumbled against her temple. "If yer mother catches us here, I'm a dead mon." He brushed the ringlets from her neck, blew on her hot skin. "We can continue this conversation later." He stepped away, then took her hand.

Kirstine took in a ragged breath and smoothed her gown, then touched her hair. "How do I look?" She didn't want to appear like a disheveled wanton.

"Like I've kissed the breath from ye," Brodie said with a hint of wonder. "Where have ye been all my life?"

"Under yer nose, ye blunderhead."

"There's my sweet lass," he said, lacing his fingers through hers. "We should have had this talk a long time ago. I swear ye ken me better than I do myself." He kissed the top of her head and drew her out into the sunshine.

They barely made it back to the edge of the crowd when Brigid spotted them. She was like a fiery tornado, clearing a path through the horde, an arm waving.

"Grandda has been look—" She narrowed her eyes, studying Kirstine, Brodie, then Kirstine again. A huge smile lit her face. "The goddess of fertility is alive and well, I see."

"Brodie needed to talk…"

"Kirsty needed to talk…"

Kirstine blushed as they both mumbled the same excuse together.

Brigid took her arm. "Go see Grandda. I'll keep Kirstine company. *We* need to talk, I'm thinking."

Kirstine's eyes followed Brodie's retreating back, the kilt hugging his hips. The soft yet sturdy material swayed against the back of his muscled legs.

"Ye finally told him?"

A grin tugged at her lips. "I did."

"I'm guessing he listened."

"He did." She gave her friend a side glance.

The sun shone copper against Brigid's hair; her blue eyes glinted with humor. "So, my brother isna as buffle-headed as he pretends. I'm happy to hear it."

"He kissed me." Kirstine was bursting. She had to tell someone. "It was as wonderful as I hoped it would be."

"I'm happy for ye, sister." Brigid gave her a hug. "So much for my matchmaking with the widower, MacDougal. It's a good thing I have other talents."

"As does your brother," Kirstine said with a giggle.

"Och, spare me the details, please," Brigid groaned. "There are some things a sister should never ken about her brother."

CHAPTER SIX
Budding Bliss or Fickle Fervor

BRODIE SHOULDERED HIS way through the men surrounding his grandfather. For the love of saints, what had just happened? Desire pounded through his veins, and he could still taste her, like the first honey of the season that stays on the lips. When he'd seen MacDougal smile down at his Kirstine... aye, *his* Kirstine.

Without thinking, he'd plowed over to the couple like a bull on a rampage. By the time he was alone with her, his blood had been up. He'd dragged her into the woods, arguing with himself over his own sanity. But those words of love had struck him hard in the chest. Her trembling lips, her heaving chest had struck other body parts. This time, he'd been helpless against his instinctive response and kissed her. Brodie had not been prepared for what happened next. The kiss had enchanted him, made him crave her touch, her taste with an intensity he'd never known before.

There is no' a mon to compare with ye.

He tried to wipe the grin from his face, but he felt so damn... happy. A woman who kept him steady and stirred his blood. Kirstine loved him, in *that* way. A month ago, he would have scoffed at the idea of returning such romantic affection. But he was a man who listened to his gut, and it told him this was right. *She* was right.

But I canna wait forever.

Those words sobered him. He was not a man who appreciated being pushed. He needed time to adjust to this revelation. But Kirstine understood him and would not nag him as other women had, his mind reasoned. Perhaps that was the magic between them. She recognized his strengths and shortcomings. Brodie would never have to play the courting games of a polite beau with her. He could be himself. Always.

"There's my grandson," declared Calum. "I have a question for ye."

He followed his grandfather away from the raucous group of men passing around flasks of whisky. "Nothing serious, I hope."

Calum shook his head. "Mairi's father asked about ye. She seems quite smitten. He hinted he would approve of a match between the two of ye if we were so inclined." His grandfather held up a hand. "I dinna want any problems with the family. They all work with us, so try to keep yer—"

"Mairi's a bonny lass," Brodie interrupted, "but something peculiar has happened since I've been back. I believe my affection has found a permanent home."

"And who might it be this time?"

"This time?"

"Aye, ye're Cupid's favorite target. I dinna have enough fingers to count how many lasses ye've fancied since ye were fifteen. A dozen cases of calf-love, at least." His grandfather grinned, but his next words were serious. "Hence, my concern with yer intentions toward Mairi."

Brodie snorted. "This is different. It's unexpected but feels right... and true."

Calum guffawed. "I've heard this before, but go ahead and surprise me. Who has stolen yer heart *this* summer?"

"Kirsty."

Calum was silent for a moment, then slapped Brodie on the back, sending him forward. "I kent it! I told yer grandmother, I said, 'Peigi, if that lad had a crumb of sense, he'd see she's wearing her heart on her sleeve.' We're both fond of the lass."

"Weel, since I have yer approval." He gave Calum a thump in return. "I'll join ye in a wee swallow."

After the festivities, Brodie rode behind the wagon, his belly full and his heart light. The leather saddle creaked beneath him as he leaned back to take in the beauty above him. The sky was a shimmery black, the stars winking at him as if they were in on his secret. Love always filled him with optimism. The anticipation of the next meeting, stolen glances and kisses, an unexpected touch that sent the heart racing and heat surging through the veins. It was unpredictable and spontaneous. The notion of being in love with Kirstine made him hard with desire. He began humming, softly at first, and then louder as his momentum grew. A verse bubbled out, and his deep voice hung on the still night air.

Like dew on the gowan lying,
Is the fall o' her fairy feet,
And like the winds in summer sighing,
Her voice is low and sweet.
Her voice is low and sweet,
And she's all the world to me…

Brigid pulled back on her reins and sidled her pony next to his. "I see ye're in fine spirits again. I'm glad she finally told ye, regardless of what happens in the future."

"Finally? How long have ye kent she had feelings for me?" His grandfather had also seemed wise to Kirstine's affection. Had he been the last to know?

"Och, brother, anyone with eyes could see she's been dangling on ye."

"Except me."

"Ye didna look. Kirsty always makes it about *ye*, and ye always let her. When was the last time ye noticed if she was Friday-faced or worried? That's right, she always puts on a smile for ye." Brigid wagged a finger at him. "Ye best no' break her heart in a month or two, or I'll come after ye myself."

Brodie guffawed. "I could take on my own sister."

"I'm just warning ye. She's one of the few females who understands me. One of the few that I call friend." Brigid gave her pony a nudge and trotted ahead to the wagon to ride beside their mother and grandmother.

The devil take him, his own sister raising a breeze about him and Kirstine. He pondered her words and his earlier conversation with Calum. Sure, he'd courted a few of the villagers. He'd never made any promises, told any bouncers to lead them on. In fact, his intentions had been pure each time that familiar surge filled his chest. He couldn't help it if the luster dulled after a month or so.

Brodie had always prided himself on remaining a gentleman. When they came to him a virgin, he left them intact. Perhaps the kisses became heated, but then, he wasn't a saint. Did Kirstine have the same opinion of him as Brigid? Did she worry his affection wouldn't last? Their kiss *had* been different. More powerful, more urgent than any he'd known before. Yet, unease chafed at his joy, a whispered warning he couldn't quite put his finger on.

Perhaps his family was right. Was he fickle? Self-centered? The revelation slapped him in the face. Yet, he was well-liked within the clans. A favorite, most said.

He remembered his mother's frequent scolding from childhood.

Ye inherited yer grandfather's charm and win the day most times. Dinna let it blind ye to yer own shortcomings.

Maybe his conversations with Kirstine *were* a bit one-sided. He thought back to one in particular.

HER FLUSHED FACE danced before him, full lips parted, chocolate eyes bright with passion. He wanted to explore these new sensations with her, discover what made her love him and why. Tomorrow was the beginning of a new adventure. And no one enjoyed a quest better than Brodie MacNaughton.

⇶⇶⇶⇷⇷⇷

THEY WERE IN the woods, kissing as they had the day before, but Brodie touched her in secret places. His fingers traced her breasts, lazily trailed down her stomach, between her legs, to cup her mound. Caressing, sliding, the friction of his touch sent currents of pleasure through her...

Kirstine threw back the counterpane, her skin damp. A dream. She clutched at her chest, willed her heartbeat to slow. Such an ardent dream.

Something clattered below. Her mother was in the kitchen preparing breakfast. The aroma of sausage wafted up to the loft, and her mouth watered. After the tryst with Brodie, she'd been too excited to eat. Her stomach gurgled, and she scrambled from the bed. Bare feet hit the thick wool rug covering the floor planks.

Kirstine poured water from the pitcher and quickly splashed her face and combed her hair. Pulling back the curtain from the tiny window, dust motes floated in the sunshine. Another beautiful day. The first day of her new life as a woman in love and Brodie loving her in return. The day she had waited for since she'd been five years old.

Dressed in her work clothes, a durable, russet wool skirt and bodice, she clambered down the ladder. Her mother's back was turned, busy cutting turnips for mashing. The rapid sound of the knife as she sliced against the scarred cutting board, matched the bob of her head. Charlie's cold nose poked at her hand, and Kirstine scratched his head.

"Ye look like a woodpecker hard at work." She giggled, kissed her mother's cheek, and grabbed a chunk of cheese. "Ye should no' have let me sleep so late. I can help ye after I gather the eggs and milk the goats."

"The turnips are almost done, but ye can start on those when ye come back." She nodded at the potatoes in a basket. "I promised yer father neeps and tatties for dinner." She looked over her shoulder. "Then ye can tell me all about yesterday while we eat breakfast."

Kirstine grinned. "Ye just want to say ye were right."

"Words a woman never hears enough," her mother agreed with a snicker.

In the smaller storage shed, she scooped some feed into her skirt, holding it out like a pocket. The hens were already out, their feathers ruffled and clucking loudly at Charlie. She scattered the seed around the yard, and their squawks ceased. Beaks blurred as they quickly pecked at the ground; their black and white feathers shimmered in the morning sun. Entering the blackhouse, she breathed in the odor of hay and manure, grabbed a basket from the mudded stone wall, and walked to the far end where the chickens were kept. There were a dozen nests for the hens, plus several roosters. The hound snuffled the straw as she filled her basket with half a dozen brown eggs, which she left at the front door for her mother.

Kirstine hummed a favorite tune as she headed out to the small pasture behind the blackhouse. The two buckets she held brushed against her skirts. The goats *baa'd* at the intrusion, but a soothing melody soon had them standing patiently while she milked them. When both buckets were half-full, she lugged them back to the house, daydreaming about her rendezvous later with Brodie. He had whispered in her ear just before they'd left the festivities last night.

"Our spot, tomorrow afternoon." His breath had been warm against her skin. *"We'll talk more then."*

She remembered the surprise in his blue eyes after their kiss. The hunger that had replaced the usual spark of humor, his lips, his hands—

"Kirstine, be careful. Ye're slopping over the sides of the pails," yelled her mother through the window.

Startled, she looked down and saw the milky liquid dribbling down her skirt. *Heavens!* she thought, *Get hold of yourself.* Her mother met her at the door and relieved her of the buckets.

"I've made extra cheese for MacDougal and his boy. He and yer father made an agreement yesterday. We'll provide them with butter, cheese, and eggs in exchange for labor." Her mother's eyes narrowed. "I suppose ye dinna want to deliver it for me now that ye've stars in yer eyes?"

"I'll do whatever ye need me to, Ma."

"Ye're a good daughter. Now, sit down and fill yer belly. We have a busy day." She filled Kirstine's bowl with porridge and placed it before her. There was already a plate of scones, toast, jam, and soft cheese on the table.

"I'm so hungry, I could have eaten the chicken feed," Kirstine said around a mouthful of toast and soft cheese. She added a dollop of honey to the porridge and then her tea. "I was too happy to eat last night."

"Tell me what happened."

Kirstine began with Brodie's jealousy at the bonfire and then his reaction after the May pole dance. While she didn't give her mother details, she admitted Brodie kissed her.

"So, he's courting ye now?"

She nodded, heat coloring her cheeks.

"Ye're sure?"

"Of course, I'm sure. I did what ye advised—told him my feelings—and he said..." What exactly had he said?

I canna deny this stirring inside me.

But he never actually said they were courting.

"I dinna want to crush yer joy, but I *will* look out for my child. I'm happy for ye, truly. Only dinna forget how fickle the mon can be. I'd hate to see ye pass up a good offer because Brodie canna decide what he wants." Her mother held up a hand when Kirstine opened her mouth to protest. "I have nothing against him. He's a MacNaughton and to be respected. I just worry he will break yer heart if he is no' serious in his affections."

She nodded, pushing away the pinprick of anxiety in her chest. "We are meeting at the swimming falls later this afternoon. I'll make sure we are of the same mind."

It turned out she didn't make a delivery to MacDougal's. Several hours later, young Liam knocked at the door. His hands were behind his back, a red curl hanging in one eye. "I come to collect, if ye please." He squinted up at her. He wiped his dirty hands on his homespun pants and offered one to her.

Kirstine accepted the handshake but doubted the boy had come by himself. "Did ye come alone?"

Liam slapped his knee and guffawed, and she wondered who he mimicked. "Me and Da are tied at the ankles, he says. We go everywhere together. He's just a wee slower than me."

"That's a long rope binding yer ankles, then." She peered around the doorway and saw MacDougal ambling up the lane. He waved, and she raised an arm in answer. "Ye should come in and have the last scone while ye wait."

"Aye, it might take him a while. Da says to have patience with old folk," he agreed with a serious face. "I dinna think I'd need so much for ye, Miss MacDunn. Ye're too bonny to be old." He wiggled onto the bench, his hands clasped on the wood table, waiting to be invited to eat.

"Ye have fine manners for no' having a mother to raise ye," Ma said from the hearth. "Go ahead, have that last bit and finish off the jam."

"Yes, ma'am." The boy's hand swiped up the scone, dipped it into the jam, and shoved it into his mouth. Sticky red smeared his lips, and a loud smacking noise came from his end of the table as he grinned and munched at the same time.

"I'm afraid ye spoke too soon," Kirstine said with a smirk.

"Liam, slow down or ye'll choke," said MacDougal from the doorway. His lanky form filled the doorway and blocked out the sun, turning his red hair a deep copper.

Kirstine had to admit, if it weren't for Brodie and the widower's gap in age, she'd be tempted. He was kind, handsome, and a good father.

"And close yer mouth when ye're chewing, son. No one wants to see yer cud." He held his cap in his hands and nodded at the women. "Please excuse Liam. We're used to eating alone and dinna always worry about proprieties."

"Nonsense, he's a good lad," disagreed her mother. "Are ye hungry? Or can I get ye some tea?"

He shook his head. "Och, no. We just left yer husband in the field and still have work at home. Perhaps another time?" His question may have been directed at Mrs. MacDunn but his pale green eyes were on *Miss* MacDunn.

"Of course, of course." The older woman handed him a burlap bag she'd filled with cheese and a small crock of butter. "Return the pot when it's empty, and I'll refill for ye."

"Who's feeling lucky?" Kirstine held up a small basket with the eggs she'd gathered earlier. She smiled as young Liam shook his head.

"Da says if there's something to break, I'll find my way to it," he proclaimed cheerfully as he left the table, wiping his mouth with his sleeve. He held out his chubby hand for the sack and tried to sling it over his shoulder.

"Easy there, lad." MacDougal caught the burlap before a mishap occurred. "Ye'll be covered in butter." He tied a knot in the material and handed it back to his son.

"Sorry, Da," he said without a hint of apology in his voice, clutching the parcel to his chest.

"Make yer polite goodbye, and we'll be off."

"Thank ye for the verra. Tasty. *Tidbit.*" Liam pronounced the words slowly then looked up at his father with a huge grin. "Did I say it right?"

"Aye, lad. Ye said it right." MacDougal gave the women a crooked smile. "We've been reading at night, and he has to practice a new word every day."

Kirstine's heart went out to the two males fending for themselves. Men weren't meant to be alone. Little boys weren't meant to be without mothers. She'd speak with Brigid about the MacDougals. Perhaps they could find someone to help the pair with some cooking and housekeeping. In the meantime, Kirstine would see what she could do for them.

One problem solved, she quickly changed her clothes to meet Brodie. She called out to her mother that she'd be back in a couple hours and ignored the older woman's snort as she skipped across the yard. After a quick stop in the drying shed, where the herbs and flowers were hung until ready, she noted what plants to keep an eye out for as she walked.

Never waste time, her grandmother had always told her, *for ye never ken how much ye have*. Kirsty still hadn't decided whether that was good advice or a morbid warning. Grandmama had been full of both.

Puffs of white cluttered the pale sky and cast rolling shadows over the glen. Her eyes swept over the varied shades of green broken by the jutting rocks. She dashed across the meadow as Charlie loped ahead of her. He paused and sniffed the air, then tipped back his head and let out a long howl. She stopped at the top of the bluff. Brodie was spread out on the boulder they used for diving, his hose and boots cast to the side. His eyes were closed, hands behind his head, and knees up. The kilt rested against his muscular thighs and her eyes were drawn to the shadow between them. Heat spread up her neck at the image of what lay beneath the material.

"Ye beat me here," she yelled to give him warning.

His eyes opened, but he didn't move. A wicked grin curved his mouth. "I missed ye."

CHAPTER SEVEN
Revelations and Romance

THE SUN WARMED his skin, and he closed his eyes, enjoying the heated rock against the bottom of his bare feet. Brodie pillowed his head with his hands and waited for Kirstine. He reflected on Calum and Brigid's words and thought of what he would say. His shock, at his feelings toward her and the unexpected certainty that they were meant to be together, had not diminished. Nor had his desire.

He'd talked to his mother before he met with Kirsty and asked how she'd known she'd found love. He'd been surprised at his mother's openness. His father had died when Brigid was only a toddler, thrown from a horse and suffered a broken neck. Brodie had known his parents were cousins. Step-cousins, to be precise. His paternal grandmother had married into the clan, bringing a young son with her.

"Yer father and I saw each other at family gatherings. We always got along well enough. I remember when I was sixteen, and they'd come for the Beltane celebration. He'd grown into a mon over the winter." His mother had sighed, a wistful smile on her face. "He'd grown tall and broad and ever so handsome."

"So ye kent right away he was the one?" Disappointment pricked Brodie's chest.

"Och no, I liked the mon, but I was courting someone else. Yer da was relentless, though, and I enjoyed the attention. He pursued me all that summer and I grew verra fond of him." She chuckled. "But I kent it was love with the first kiss."

Brodie smiled. His mother's words had given him confidence. He and Kirstine were friends who cared about one another and trusted each other. It was a good foundation. They'd been raised with similar philosophies and looked at life much the same way. A shout interrupted his rumination, and he looked up to see a shaggy hound and a bonny lass, tail and arms waving at him from above.

"I'll meet ye up there," he called back as he put his boots back on and jumped from the boulder.

Scaling the hill, he found Kirstine under their tree, the plaid already spread on the damp earth. She smiled, the same smile he'd known for fifteen years but with an added question in her eyes. He'd have to remove that. Charlie thumped his tail where he lay several feet away.

Brodie stepped onto the blanket and reached for her hand. She stared at the blanket, suddenly shy. He lifted her chin, but his smile faded when his eyes locked on her trembling lips. Brushing his mouth against hers, her sigh warmed his skin, and a *thrum* started low in his belly.

He pulled her close, his arms around her waist, their bodies snug against each other. Her body molded to his as if they'd been two halves separated during another lifetime and finally found each other. He dipped his head again and pressed his lips to hers, his tongue sweeping the seam of her mouth. She tasted of heather tea and honey. His heart ached with the sweetness of her while his mind wondered why this had taken them so long. He pulled away reluctantly.

"As ye can see, I havena changed my mind," he murmured against her hair. "But we need to talk."

Kirstine nodded, her dark eyes bright. They sat down on the plaid, and he leaned back on his elbows with his ankles crossed. She did the same while they both studied the landscape. The waterfall gurgled and splashed. The sun peeked out from behind a cloud, and the spray glistened and sparkled as it hit the clear stream. The rays snaked between the dense cluster of branches and cast speckles of light across their bodies and the plaid. Birds chirped above them, and the earthy smell of pine and soil soothed his jumbled thoughts.

"What's going through yer head right now?" He tried to remember the speech he'd planned.

"The truth?" she asked without her usual humor.

"Of course. When have ye given me anything else?" His stomach tightened a bit at her tone. It didn't sound like a woman who'd just been thoroughly kissed.

"I see the same expression in yer eye now that I've seen a dozen times before. Each time ye find someone new, ye get that glazed look, like the stained glass of the church when the sun's rays come through. All bright and hazy."

"That's no' true, Kirsty." He stopped when she held up a hand.

"I dinna want to be another one of yer cast-offs. So, I'm giving ye the chance to end this now before it ruins our friendship. We can forget this ever happened if I'm only to be yer next summer love." Her words were harsh, but tears shimmered in her eyes. "I couldna bear it."

Her words punched him in the gut. "So ye have the same opinion of me as my grandfather and sister?"

"I'm no' sure what ye mean." Her gaze was fixed ahead, watching a hawk perch on a spindly pine growing from the side of the cliff.

"That I'm inconstant, my affection wanders easily." A small knot replaced the punch.

She shook her head. "I think ye love to fall in love. It's the excitement of someone new that lures ye, the chase. And once it's over, so are yer affections."

Brodie mulled this over. She was right, of course. The first flutters of new love were like a good scotch whisky. A slow, intoxicating burn that spread through his limbs and down the body. How could he explain to her that this was different?

"If this doesna work out between us, we canna return to the way things were. Is that what ye're saying?"

When she nodded, he swallowed the lump in his throat. Losing Kirstine's friendship was not a possibility. She was a part of his life, in his daily thoughts, his support. He needed her like roots needed soil. He hadn't made an important decision without her since he was ten years old.

"And if we stop now, we can continue as we have been?"

Kirstine hesitated, then gave him another nod.

"What will ye do then?" he asked, though he knew the answer.

"I will consider courtship and marriage with another."

"To the likes of MacDougal?" The knot twisted and grew.

"It doesna matter *who*, Brodie. I am almost one and twenty and must consider my future. My ma is right. I willna be happy without a family of my own." She blew out a long breath. "Ye will always be in my heart, ye ken that, but I must move forward. This limbo I've put myself in is no' working anymore."

Was this an ultimatum? It ruffled his pride that she would push him into a corner. That was what usually ended his dalliances. "So, I need to decide if I want to marry ye this very minute or forfeit the chance?"

Kirstine stood and brushed off her wool skirt. His eyes lingered on her backside.

"I never said anything about betrothals today, but this *is* about commitment. Let's meet again tomorrow, and ye can reflect on what I've said." She moved off the plaid.

He was on his feet quicker than a frog on a fly. The sudden motion brought Charlie to his feet, watching Brodie with narrowed golden eyes. He snorted at the hound's possessiveness. Well, that made two of them.

"I dinna need a day to consider my life without ye." He caught her arm and turned her to face him.

"Ye tend to be impulsive when it comes to love, Brodie. It's the only time yer brain doesna mull a subject over to see every viewpoint and implication." She threw her hands in the air. "It's as if ye're blind on the matter. Ye leap first and see where ye land after ye've fallen."

"I ken where I'm falling right now. Exactly where fate has wanted me to be these past ten years." Brodie cupped her face, his thumb brushing away a tear. "My grandfather and sister have the same worries, so I'm no' hearing these sentiments for the first time. But this *is* different. Ye fill a void no other can. It just took me a wee longer to figure it out."

An image of MacDougal filled his mind, his hand on Kirstine's lower back as he led her to the May pole. Brodie's gentleness vanished. His mouth claimed hers hungrily; he parted her lips with his tongue and swept inside. When her arms draped around his neck, his fingers threaded into her silky tresses, one hand moving down her back to cup her buttocks. He feathered kisses across her jaw, hard with desire as her head fell back, exposing her neck. His lips worked their way down, paused at the hollow in her throat, then traced along her collarbone with his tongue.

Her gasp brought him from the fog. For the love of saints, he wanted to take her right here. He stepped back, grasped her arms, but kept a space between their bodies. They stood panting, their eyes locked.

"I love ye, Brodie MacNaughton." Her fingers dug into his forearms, her chest heaving. "Promise me ye willna break my heart." Her eyes were dark and pleading, her voice breaking.

He tucked a burnished red strand behind her ear. She'd never looked so lovely. "I promise no' to break yer heart, Kirsty." He gathered her in a tight hug. She clung to him, and he marveled at the certainty that invaded his soul. "Can we still meet tomorrow?"

She giggled into his chest, but her head moved in agreement. Then she pushed at his chest until he was off the blanket. From years of habit, they each took an end of the plaid, shook it, and came together, then repeated the actions until it was folded in a tight square. Brodie wrapped the cover around it and tucked it back into its hiding place in the branch. They descended the hill and left the wood together, Charlie loping in front.

When he got back to the castle, his mother called for him. As usual, Glynnis was busy sewing... something. The woman was never idle. It seemed to be a MacNaughton trait.

"Ian will be home in a few days," she announced, beaming. "Lissie has already started baking in the kitchen. The mon will have a stomach the size of a sow by the time he returns to Glasgow."

Ian's wife, Lissie, retreated to her culinary sanctuary whenever she needed to take her mind off a worry. Or was angry and needed to punch some dough. Or bored. Or happy that her husband was coming home. It had taken their cook, Enid, a bit of adjustment to have another female in and out of her kitchen. One who wasn't there to do her bidding.

Brodie paused, his hand to his ear. "Och, I can hear Enid mumbling under her breath from here. I should go keep the peace."

"Stop, now. Dinna cause trouble where there's no' any," his mother admonished good-naturedly. "Besides, ye only want to see what ye can swipe."

"It's worth it when I dinna get caught." He rubbed his belly. "I'm as starved as a lost sheep in winter."

"Aye, ye look a bit scrawny. Where have ye been?" Her needle paused mid-air to give him a sideways glance, then she chuckled. "Ah, I see."

Brodie opened his mouth to argue but knew it was pointless. He wasn't sure what irritated him more—that his mother assumed she knew his mind or that she was almost always right in her assumptions.

BRODIE BALANCED HIS weight against the roof and the ladder. The sun beat down on them, and he blinked at the sweat stinging his eye. He wiped a forearm over his face, clearing away the straw dust mixed with perspiration that covered his bared chest and arms. It had been a long week, but the re-thatch on the blacksmith's cottage was almost finished. Below, one man bundled straw while MacDougal met Brodie halfway up the ladder with a finished bunch. Brodie fixed it next to the others, completing the last section, and pushed a large V-shaped peg over the bundle to hold it in place. MacDougal tossed up a long stick to secure the row of bundles. The *snip* of shears sounded as the thatcher trimmed the edges of the roof that had been completed.

The first couple days had been awkward as Brodie tried to avoid MacDougal. Not sure how the widower felt about Kirstine, he hadn't wanted to appear smug. But the man was congenial and a hard worker. At the end of the second workday, they'd had a nip together, and the unease had disappeared. Brodie liked the man and his son, though the boy tended to be constantly underfoot.

By the third day, Glynnis took pity on the men and asked Liam to help her with some very important chores. Giving the boy her full attention, she would take his hand and listen patiently to his endless questions and narrative on life. Brodie remembered that same attentiveness when he used to regale her with the number of types of insects he'd found in the wood. Or why a tadpole down his sister's shirt was an experiment to see how high she could jump rather than a devious plot to watch her rant.

He glanced at his brother, Ian, who was wiping his face with his shirttail. Aye, his mother would welcome a grandchild.

"Is anyone hungry?" Glynnis called from the yard. "I've brought some cold meat pies and strawberries."

"And I sliced bread and cut cheese, *and* I carried one of the baskets," spouted Liam.

"Ye're a saint, Ma," called Brodie as he descended the ladder and kissed her on the cheek. She handed him a mug of water, which he promptly poured over his head. The cool liquid streamed down his face and back, then trickled under his kilt. He leaned over and shook his hair, spraying everything and everyone within his vicinity.

"Ye've been doing that since ye were a lad." Glynnis laughed.

"He's got the manners of Da's hound," groused Ian, coming from the other side of the cottage. He stood next to Brodie, a taller and leaner version of his younger brother.

"Speaking of beasties," Brodie mused, "didn't I hear Brownie's howl earlier?" Their oldest brother's deerhound had put up quite a fuss when Lachlan left her behind. His mother said the hound's wails had been unbearable. She'd slept in Brigid's room the first night and had not left the girl's side since.

"I'll take a cup, too, please. I'm parched." Ian tipped back his head, his Adam's apple bobbing up and down as he finished off the water in one long drink. "Aye, that was Brownie. Brigid tried to leave her here and go down to the stream for more water, but the yowls began. If only Lachlan could find a woman as devoted as his canine."

Brodie laughed. "I dinna see that happening in the near future."

"Perhaps no' in Lachlan's future." Ian wiggled his dark brows. "But I hear there's been a wee romance blooming with our Kirsty."

Brodie thanked the sun for already turning his face red. He opened his mouth to make a clever retort, but his sister yelled from the edge of the wood.

Brownie loped in front, Brigid trailing behind with a long thin branch bowed across her shoulders and two buckets balanced on either end. Strands of auburn locks had fallen from her bun, streaked red by the afternoon light as she trudged across the grass. Water sloshed over the sides, and Brodie could hear Brigid's mumbled curse.

"Brigid Mary!" yelled Glynnis, putting her hands over the younger MacDougal's ears. "I canna believe ye'd eat with the same mouth."

Little Liam pulled the older woman's hands away. "Och, ma'am, I've heard worse from my da."

All eyes turned to MacDougal, who had just finished a drink and wiped his mouth on his shirt sleeve. "Son, be still. The ladies will assume we have no decorum."

"But Da, when the hen got yer finger yesterday, ye called her a worthless piece of fe—"

"Go help Miss Brigid with those buckets. They look a wee heavy for the poor lass." MacDougal stared at his cup, then peeked up at Glynnis. "My apologies to the lady present."

"Och, none needed," she said with a smile. "Two men alone have no reason to guard their tongue. I think ye're doing a fine job with the boy."

"I appreciate that, ma'am. And thank ye again for yer help with him this week while we worked." He nodded at Glynnis, and she smiled in return, her eyes crinkling with pleasure.

Brodie watched the exchange between the two of them. For a moment, his mother looked years younger. Then Liam shouted, catching the attention of all the adults.

The boy jumped and tried to tap one of the buckets. It teetered for a moment, splashing the excited child. He squealed and jumped again, ignoring Brigid's thunderous words of caution and the vigorous shake of her head. On the second try, his fingers hooked the top of the bucket. Brigid tried to pull down on the opposite side of the stick to balance the weight of both boy and pail, but the first bucket slid off. The group froze, mouths open, as the second pail slid down the pole and dumped its contents over Brigid. She gasped, tripped, and stumbled forward, taking Liam down with her.

Sprawled out on the grass with a pole on top of her back, a boy doubled over with laughter next to her, and a hound licking at her face, Brigid let out a torrent of unintelligible words. Brodie clamped his mouth shut, holding back his guffaws as he locked eyes with his little sister. Och, it was good that boy wasn't related to her, or she'd have a piece of his hide.

Liam looked back at the group and waved at Glynnis. "Not to worry, ma'am. Still nothing I've no' heard before."

CHAPTER EIGHT
The Courtship Commences

K IRSTINE HEARD THE happy shriek of a child, followed by loud female cursing. She cringed, recognizing Brigid's voice, and wondered what kind of mischief the young MacDougal had caused. When she came out of the wood, giggles bubbled up her throat.

Brigid lay flat on the grass, her skirts hitched above her ankle. A long, crooked branch trapped her and Liam to the ground. The older needed to be rescued. The younger was having a tremendous time laughing and poking at the victim next to him. Brownie hunched over both of them, licking one face and then another. Two buckets were scattered on either side, and as Kirstine drew closer, she could see they once held water. Much of the liquid now appeared to be worn by the two struggling bodies trapped beneath the furry hound.

A group from the cottage ran to help, but the three MacNaughtons stopped short and leaned on each other while they clutched their bellies. Snorts and cackles filled the air. A cautious MacDougal braved the ire of Brigid and extricated her from the pole, the dog, and the boy.

"Saints and sinners," grumbled Brigid. "Does the entire glen need to witness my downfall?"

Glynnis rolled her eyes. "Only yer pride is hurt, lass. And the sun will dry those clothes in the blink of an eye." She narrowed her eyes at the youth. "As far as ye're concerned, Mr. MacDougal, I'm fairly certain ye'll no' be laughing soon enough."

The boy looked up at his father, then back at Glynnis. His eyes grew wide as he realized *he* was the Mr. MacDougal is question, not his father. With his hands clasped behind his back and a whistle on his lips, he took one step back. As he turned on his heel, Liam caught the boy by his collar and pulled him up. Bare feet kicked at the air and his high-pitched yelp sent Brownie into a howling frenzy.

"I believe it's time to take our leave before ye create another catastrophe." MacDougal set his son down. "Now apologize to the lady, and the rest of the group, for yer mischief. And we'll finish this conversation at home."

Liam hung his head, toes digging into the grass, and mumbled, "I'm verra sorry, Miss Brigid. I didna mean to cause ye to fall."

"I accept yer apology. Next time, listen to an adult's warning." Brigid ruffled his hair. "The water did feel fine on such a hot day."

He looked up with a grin, his tongue showing through a missing front tooth. "Happy to oblige."

The two MacDougals climbed in their wagon, and Brodie moved beside Kirstine as they waved goodbye. She tried not to look at the bare chest next to her, but her eyes didn't obey. He'd tossed a towel over his shoulder, evidently to dry himself off. Her gaze tracked a drop of water making its way down the center of his stomach. Her finger itched to stop it, taste the salt from his skin.

Ye're a wanton woman, Kirstine MacDunn, she scolded herself.

"What have ye been up to, my bonny Kirsty?" asked Brodie in a husky voice.

His breath was hot against her skin, and the flush on her cheeks had nothing to do with the sun.

"I'm on an errand for more beeswax. On the way home, I thought I'd stop and see yer progress." She sucked in a breath, his fragrant mix of pine and sweat, a heady combination. "Almost finished, then?"

He nodded, his hand resting on her lower back as he steered her back toward the cottage. "Are ye out of candles?"

She paused at the question, then laughed. "No, we use the wax to make ointments. Summer is my busiest season, as it is for all healers. Many of the plant parts we need for the tinctures and infusions are gathered ahead of time for winter."

"Yer busy season? But yer mother is the healer, ye just help—"

Kirstine stopped and planted her fists on her hips. Where had he been all these years? "Do ye pay attention to anything that doesna concern ye in particular? What have I been doing with my mother all these years?"

"Assisting?" His blue eyes sparkled as he took in her stance, a smile creeping around the edges of his mouth. He ducked when she took a flimsy swipe at him.

"Numpty-headed mon," she mumbled, walking away from him. Over her shoulder, she yelled, "I've been learning. I will be a second healer for the clan *and* a midwife. I've helped with two births in the past year."

"Ye're lovely when ye're angry. Did ye ken that?" he called after her.

Bare chest or no, the man was still infuriating.

"Don't pay him any mind, lass," said Glynnis. "My son can still be a wee self-centered, but ye'll shape him into a good mon, eventually."

"Ye have too much in faith in me."

"I have faith in love. He loves ye." Glynnis smiled. "And a mon will do anything within reason for the woman he loves."

Heat spread up Kirstine's neck at the words. "Do ye think—"

"No talking behind my back unless I can hear what's said," interrupted Brodie as he approached.

"Turn yer back, and I promise we'll talk louder," quipped his mother.

He snorted. "Grandda taught me better than to turn my back on a wily adversary."

Both women beamed.

"I'll take that as a compliment," Glynnis retorted. "Now go and walk yer pretty lass home. Ian will drive me in the wagon."

"Aye, we're done for the day. I canna help trim the roof edge without the proper tools." Brodie held out his hand, and she took it, twining her fingers with his.

The *snip* of the thatcher's shears faded as they made their back through the woods and toward Kirstine's home. Once in the shadows, his arm looped around her back and pulled her close. His lips grazed her neck, then captured her mouth, his tongue velvet against hers. Her palms lay flat on his chest. His *bare* chest. She moaned as her stomach tumbled and her fingertips kneaded Brodie's solid muscle. How could his skin feel so supple yet so hard at the same time? She ran her nails against the springy dark curls that tapered down his stomach.

"That was better than the cold meat pie Ma brought us." He rested his forehead on hers, his hands stroking her back lightly. Pleasure rippled through her. "And I was hungry, so ye must be verra tasty."

Kirstine giggled, stood on her tiptoes, and bit his lower lip. "No dallying this afternoon. I have too much to do at home." She pushed away from him and resumed walking, swinging her sack of beeswax.

Brodie untied the shirt from his waist and pulled it over his head. "I suppose I should look presentable in front of yer mother."

She bent her head but peeked at him through her lashes as he covered the smooth tanned skin. He was a beautiful specimen of a man.

"I see ye watching, Kirsty."

Embarrassed, she turned on her heel, picking up speed and emerging from the wood into the bright sunshine. She grabbed her skirts with one hand and took off at a run. Behind her, Brodie followed with whoops of laughter.

"Ye can run but ye canna hide, love," he called. "I will always find ye."

They ran across the emerald meadow, a hawk in full spread gliding above to cast a flittering shadow over their path. At a row of hedges with sweet-scented white flowers, Kirstine stopped and caught her breath. She motioned Brodie to the privet bushes. Opening the drawstring pouch at her waist, she withdrew a small knife and began cutting the white flowers.

"I appreciate the gesture, fair lady, but I should be the one presenting you with a posy." He crossed his arms and grinned at her. "But if ye're one of those independent lasses, I'll graciously accept."

She rolled her eyes and handed him her sack. "We add the flowers to sweet water or tea. It helps with any disease that needs cooling or drying. And fluxes of the belly and..." Brodie didn't want to know about women's menses. "They'll no' be in bloom much longer, so I like to gather as many as I can when I come across them. Then we'll collect the berries in late summer."

"And what kind of potion do ye make with the berries?"

"Their ideal for washing sores when made into a lotion."

"I'm impressed with what ye ken about these things." He squinted into the bag as she carefully laid the blossoms inside the pouch. "Who have ye helped with yer healing, Kirsty? Tell me about yer work."

She paused, a smile tugging at her lips at his request. Perhaps Glynnis was right. Her Brodie was making an effort to be attentive. She retrieved the sack and placed the last petals inside, along with the blade, and tied the laces to her belt.

"The first serious patient I remember," she began, not counting the goat she'd found at the age of seven, "was the shopkeeper in the village. He'd fallen from a ladder while stocking his shelves. His leg was broken, and his shoulder dislocated."

"I remember that. It took him months to recover," added Brodie. "Grandda worried he'd ever be the same."

"Ma taught me how to put the shoulder back into its rightful place.

The mon was in terrible pain but never made a sound." She grimaced. "I suspect he didna want to frighten his new wife."

"Is it a difficult procedure?"

She shook her head. "Ye need strength, though. I couldna have done it when I was younger. And ye must do it as quickly as possible. The longer it takes, the more pain to the patient."

"What else have ye done?"

"Let's see. I've assisted with several births, but I believe I could deliver a bairn on my own if there were no complications. I've attended those with fever or flux, sewed up several long gashes—"

"Ye've stitched a mon? With a needle?" His azure eyes widened. It was a well-known fact that Brodie hated needles.

She chortled. "Careful, ye're turning green."

"Aye, right." He gave an exaggerated shiver. "I get lightheaded just imagining a needle poking into my skin."

"Remember when Brigid fell from her pony and hit her head? My mother gave her close to a dozen stitches."

"I recall her tumbling from the horse but no' the surgery."

"She never made a sound, not even a whimper." Kirstine poked him in the stomach. "You, on the other hand, swooned and yer brother had to catch ye before ye hit the floor."

"We all have our Achilles' heel," Brodie grumbled, then grinned. "But I never scream and do a jig when a spider drops from a tree."

It was her turn to shiver. "I concede. Everyone has a weakness."

He took her hand again and pulled her onto the dirt lane. "Do ye see that as yer purpose, then? To take yer mother's place some day?"

She nodded. "Healing is in my soul. When I help someone who suffers from illness or injury, it fills a part of me that nothing else does. It's my calling, just as yours is to be chief when the time comes."

"So, ye believe in fate?" His gaze traveled her face, the humor gone from his tone. "That we all have a predestined role to play in this life?"

"Why, Brodie MacNaughton, what has ye so philosophical today?"

"I want to be a better mon for ye, Kirsty. I want to be the one ye bring yer problems to, the one ye trust with yer deepest secrets." He let out a long, ragged sigh. "But I need to ask and listen instead of doing all the talking. I'm no' fickle, not really. My loyalty to this clan never wavers."

"No one doubts that, Brodie." Granted, his romantic affections rose and fell like the tide. But his allegiance, his place within his family, were a source of pride. The love of family and clan had always been strong and steady.

But could he transfer that kind of devotion to her, to one woman? Her mother said time would tell, but she didn't need time. "I have faith in ye, and that will never change. Ye ken that, right?"

He shrugged, and she swore a blush crept up his neck. "I dreamt ye married MacDougal and woke up this morning in a sweat. It had me pondering... if ye hadn't kissed me on May Day, would we have had another chance? Or would I have lost ye and never ken what I was missing?"

She was enjoying this new courtship and found herself in no hurry to end it. It would be a rousing summer, and she would relish every precious moment of it. "Fated to disregard the allusive love drifting before yer eyes?"

"Ye're teasing me now." He tipped his head, squinting at her suspiciously.

Kirstine shook her head. Her heart swelled as she realized there were still a few secrets hidden inside this complex man. "Truly, I trust that if we keep an open mind and an open heart, what is meant to be will come to pass. It's those who fight their destiny that lose their way."

Brodie nodded. "Lovely and clever. How did I get so lucky?"

She studied his profile, the set jaw, the forehead puckered in concentration. "What else is on yer mind?"

He shrugged again and then let out a long breath. "Ye've taught me something new about myself. I have a jealous vein I didna ken I had. When I saw ye with MacDougal, I-I wanted to skelp his hide. I dinna care for the tightness in my chest or the fire in my gut when his hand was on yer back."

"It's a good thing he's no' as handsome as ye, then."

"*As* handsome?" His fingers gripped hers. "Ye see him like that?"

"Aye, and plenty of others. There's been lots of nattering about his need for a wife and mother for the boy." Kirstine's eyes narrowed. "No confrontations with him, Brodie."

His arm snaked around her waist and they continued walking. "I hate to admit it, but I like him. He's a good mon and a hard worker. Though, the laddie could do with some restraint."

She snorted. "Like ye had any at his age."

"True enough." He studied a fluffy white cloud overhead. "What about Brigid? Maybe yer sly matchmaker should consider him for herself. It would do her good to settle down and practice more womanly duties."

Kirstine caught his gaze, and they stared at each other for a moment, then burst into laughter.

"Someday, a man will sweep her off her feet." Kirstine caught her breath. "The right man, who understands her ways, could convince her to let her feminine side come out to play."

"As ye understand my ways?"

She nodded, her eyes tracing the square line of his jaw, the dark stubble against the tanned skin.

"Is that what a woman wants? To be swept off her feet?" asked Brodie. "For the love of saints, I had no idea it was so simple."

Before she could blink, he'd swept her into his arms and twirled her round and round. She clutched his neck to keep her balance and allowed the giggles to erupt. When Brodie stopped spinning, the world did not. She focused on the stormy blue of his eyes as he kissed her. Soft, gentle, teasing. This time her head spun but for an entirely different reason.

"Yes," she said and promptly hiccupped. "This is exactly what a woman wants."

CHAPTER NINE
Feed a Fever, Stoke a Scot

June 1819

"**H**ELP! MRS. MACDUNN, please, help!"

The shrill panic in that voice and Charlie's excited bark spurred Kirstine to the window. Beyond the blackhouse, Mairi stumbled up the slight incline. The goats scampered out of her way, bleating with indignation.

Kirstine met her in the yard and caught her friend by the shoulders. "Breathe," she commanded in a calm voice.

Mairi gulped in deep breaths, her fingers digging into Kirstine's arm. "My grandmother," she huffed.

"What's happened?"

"Fever." She dragged in another breath. "She's delirious. It's getting worse."

"Come in and sit down while I collect a few things. Ye'll no' be any help if ye canna walk or talk."

Nodding, Mairi followed her in the house. "Where's Mrs. MacDunn?"

"My mother's gone into Dunderave with my da, but I've assisted her since I was eight." She squeezed her friend's shoulder. "I'll leave a note, and I'll send Charlie back if we need help. Do ye trust me?"

Mairi's shimmering gaze locked with hers as a tear slipped down her cheek. She nodded, her bright red hair a mass of tangled, frizzy curls.

"Good. Now, tell me when she came down with the fever."

Kirstine listened and asked several more questions, ascertaining what tinctures or poultices might be needed. Agnes hadn't been well the day before and retired early. This morning she'd slept late, and Mairi had busied herself with the daily chores. When she returned, she found her father frantic because of her grandmother's deteriorating condition.

"I'm going to the shed for a few more supplies. We can take old Captain and ride double." Her pony Speckles would be much quicker, but she hesitated to leave Mairi behind. The poor thing was exhausted and would worry all the way home.

Fever could mean illness or infection. Injury didn't seem to be the cause, but Kirstine wanted to be prepared. This would be the first emergency she'd handled alone. Quickly choosing another bottle and a tin, she added them to her mother's satchel and emerged into the afternoon sunlight. Charlie was barking again, and a shadowed figure loomed above her on horseback.

"Oh, Brodie. I'm so sorry, but I canna meet with ye today. Mairi's grandmother is ill."

Mairi came from the back of the blackhouse, leading Captain.

"I hope it's no' serious. She'll be dead before ye arrive if ye take that ancient mount. Is yer pony lame?"

She shook her head and explained.

"I'll accompany ye and the lass can ride behind me." He handed Kirstine his reins. "Wait here. I'll saddle yer horse for ye."

Brodie approached Mairi, spoke to her, and she nodded. He led the gelding back and soon returned with the spotted pony. He handed the bag to Mairi and gave Kirstine a leg up, then mounted his own horse.

Mairi grabbed his outstretched arm, and he swung her up and behind him. With the satchel between the two of them, she wrapped her arms firmly around his waist.

"Are we ready, ladies?" he asked, all humor gone from his tone.

"Aye," they both said in unison and set off at a gallop, the deer-hound racing alongside them.

Mairi's father, Sean, met them at the door, his hazel eyes blood-shot and tired. He ran a hand through his auburn hair. "She's mumbling about faeries and seeing her daughter again."

"Brodie, would ye see to the horses while Mairi and I tend to Ag-nes?" She laid a hand on Sean's shoulder. "Go on now, and we'll take over. Ye look worn out."

He nodded. "I dinna ken what we'll do without her. She's been a second mother to me. When my wife died, she swooped in like an angel and…" Sean swiped a calloused hand over his face. "Please, help her… help us."

Kirstine followed Mairi into a small chamber at the back of the cottage. The room was stifling. "Lord have mercy, it's hot enough for the devil himself. Open the window so we can all breathe!"

A gentle gust brought immediate relief as Kirstine pulled back the counterpane. She could feel the heat emanating from the fragile body. The elderly woman's nightshift was soaked, loose tendrils of her silver hair sticking to her crepe-like skin. When she opened her eyes, they were dark and glazed. Her head tossed back and forth against the damp pillow.

"Agnes, can ye hear me?" she asked. A bony hand gripped her arm, but there was no response.

"Let's get her undressed and find clean sheets for her to lie on. We'll cool her down with lavender water and see what ails her." It would be a long night. Fevers were unpredictable and could last hours or days. Kirstine prayed there was no rash beneath the nightrail.

Brodie appeared at the door with a bucket of cold water. "Can I help?"

She shook her head. "Stay with Sean, distract him. I'll come out after I've examined her."

In a steady, composed voice, she spoke to Mairi as she withdrew a bottle and cloths from the satchel. She added the tincture to the bucket of water and put the girl to work, making strips and soaking them in the lavender water. Mairi's face relaxed as she set about her task.

Keep them busy, give the family members a purpose. There's less time to worry, and it eases the sense of helplessness. It had been one of the first lessons her mother had given.

As they bathed Agnes, the elderly woman quieted. Kirstine washed and inspected her frail form, looking for a clue as to what had caused the fever. She pulled away the damp sheet to sponge Agnes's legs.

"Mairi, what happened to her foot?" Kirstine gingerly touched the swollen appendage. A dark bluish purple with yellow pus oozed from between several toes.

"She was milking the cow last week and got stepped on. I noticed her limp didna improve, but she told me it was fine." Mairi's green eyes darkened in horror. "I had no idea. Oh, sweet Jesu!"

"It's no' yer fault. She's a stubborn woman. But this may be the reason for her fever." Kirsten took a deep breath and got to work. "While I attend the foot, could ye continue the fresh strips across her brow and chest to keep her cool? Sprinkle some on the pillow. The scent is soothing."

Mairi nodded, and Kirstine returned to her inspection. Only one toe seemed broken, but the skin was badly ripped. The laceration had festered. With a prayer of thanks that the patient was unconscious, she carefully debrided the wound. "Hand me that brown bottle, please."

Mairi hurried over and hovered, wringing her hands. Kirstine cleaned the area with a lotion made from privet leaves. Then she made a poultice of honey and yarrow.

"This will continue to draw out any infection," she said as she bandaged the foot. "And now we wait and pray. Ye might want to put the kettle on."

By evening, the patient had managed to drink some tea with a willow bark tincture and was resting comfortably. Kirstine leaned back against the rocker and smiled. Satisfaction settled in her belly as she watched the steady rise and fall of Agnes's chest. Mairi had lit a fire and a soft yellow glow filled the room.

"My mother will return tomorrow and change the bandage. She'll want to inspect the wound herself. In the meantime, continue to bathe her with the sweet water if she becomes restless. Give her more willow bark tincture when she wakes and some beef tea or barley gruel when she can eat." Kirstine stood and stretched, feeling the dull ache in her lower back. "As long as we can keep the infection under control, she should recover."

Mairi hurried around the bed and threw her arms around Kirstine. "Thank ye again. She's as much my ma as she is my grandmother. I'd be lost without her," she sniffled.

"I'm happy to help."

"Ye were so capable and self-assured." Mairi stepped back and squeezed Kirstine's hand. "I can see why Brodie chose ye over me."

Kirstine drew in her breath. "Mairi—"

"Go on, now. He's waiting for ye."

"Brodie?"

Mairi nodded. "He said he'd no' leave without ye. Been sitting with Da all this time, keeping his mind off…" Her eyes shone, and she dashed away a tear. "But we can walk out with a smile on our faces now and put his fears to rest." She gave Kirstine another quick hug and slipped out of the room.

Kirstine collected her things and fastened the satchel. She was bone-tired. Sean wrapped her in a bear hug, and she thought she'd swoon from the lack of air.

"I swear, Miss MacDunn, ye've earned a few more steps toward the pearly gates this day. We'll no' forget what ye've done for us."

Her eyes settled on Brodie's solid form, his shoulder against the doorframe, arms crossed over his broad chest. She self-consciously smoothed her rumpled skirt, but the concern in his gaze warmed her. When he reached out and laced his fingers through hers, it didn't matter. She wanted to melt against him and sleep for a day and a night.

They walked outside, and Kirstine breathed in the crisp night air as Brodie fetched the horses. Charlie appeared from the shadows, then licked her hand. She scratched his wiry fur and talked to him softly as his tail made a soft, rhythmic *thump* against the dirt. She forced her eyes to remain open, wondering how she'd stay awake on the ride home. But it turned out, she didn't need to. Brodie came around, tied her satchel to Speckles, then lifted her onto his horse. He climbed up behind her and pulled her body against his hard chest, placing Speckles' reins in her hand to pony the horse behind them. One muscled arm rested protectively over her stomach, and Kirstine could feel the pulse of his neck against the crown of her head as she settled back. With a satisfied sigh, she allowed the exhaustion to take over. Brodie's strength enveloped her, keeping her safe.

"I'm worried ye might fall off yer spirited beastie. Yer lids look as heavy as stones. So close yer eyes, and I'll keep ye safe." He kissed the top of her head and clucked to his gelding, the pony plodding beside them. "I had no idea ye were so knowledgeable in… I'm verra proud of ye, Kirsty."

She smiled sleepily and snuggled into his warmth. Brodie had waited for her. And recognized her talent as a healer. *Merciful heavens, could I love this man any more?* She drifted off to the steady *clip clop* of the horse's hooves, sheltered in his embrace.

BRODIE SMILED AS her body relaxed against him, her breathing steady.

Goosebumps rose on her bare skin from the chilly night air. He pulled his plaid around her and chuckled to the myriad of stars glittering above them. As she fidgeted in her sleep, his hold tightened around her slight form. The curve of her hips fit perfectly between his thighs, her belly soft against his forearm.

He'd never seen her in this capacity. Someone with a skill, with authority. Poor Sean had been beside himself, and Mairi in tears. Kirstine had blanketed the entire cottage with her calm efficiency and straightforward manner. She'd set everyone to work and kept their minds occupied on a task rather than the *what ifs* of the sick room. Her tone had been quiet but determined, infusing hope in those around her. It was a gift, really, that ability not only to tend and comfort the ailing but also soothe a family's anxiety.

He nuzzled his cold nose in her silky chestnut hair. Citrus and vanilla. Tart yet sweet. That certainly described his Kirsty. It seemed the girl he'd known all his life had grown into a complicated and enticing woman.

When they reached the MacDunn property, he saw the flicker of a lantern in the front window. Charlie trotted ahead, probably nosing around for the supper he'd missed. Her folks would be worried. It had been mid-afternoon when they'd ridden pell-mell from here. It must be close to midnight now.

Brodie brushed the hair back from her face and feathered kisses down her neck. "Wake up, love," he leaned down and whispered.

His breath must have tickled, for she made a groggy noise and swatted at her ear. Her finger jammed into his eye, pain exploding in the socket.

"Bloody hell," he yelled as his hand flew to his face.

Kirsty jerked awake. Her head snapped back and connected hard with his chin.

"For the love of saints," he groaned through clenched teeth.

Her bottom ground against his crotch as she squirmed to turn around. He closed his eyes and held his breath.

"Where am—what did—Oh!" She stilled, her fingers covering her lips. "Ye're bleeding."

"Aye. Now I ken if ye're ever kidnapped, it's the bandit I'll be sorry for." His tongue traced the swell of his lower lip, then he moved his jaw back and forth.

Kirsty wiped a tear from his watering eye. "Do ye still think I'm a good healer?" she asked. Her gaze glittered black under the yellow moon, lips upturned impishly.

"I'd rather ye show me." His voice sounded gruff as he fought to control the throb low in his belly. "Take away my pain, Kirsty."

Passion replaced the fading smile. Her finger tenderly traced the side of his face. She sat up to kiss his temple, then his good eye, and made her way down his jaw to his mouth. He closed his eyes and stifled the groan scratching at his throat.

Velvet lips brushed the corner of his mouth, his chin, then stopped at the bruise. Her tongue skimmed over the battered lip before she kissed the other corner of his mouth. He lost the battle and moaned, knew she had to feel his stiffness against her side.

She leaned back, their breaths mingling in the air between them. When he opened his eyes, Kirsty winked at him.

"I believe my job is done here." One more quick kiss and her hand slid down his chest and across his lap. She slid from the horse, collected Speckles, and trotted across the yard.

"Aye, right," he croaked and rubbed his chin to keep his hand from cradling his crotch, then winced. With a chuckle, he turned the gelding and headed home. A deep contented guffaw soon turned into a gut-splitting belly laugh. "Where have ye been all my life, Kirsty Mac-Dunn?" he shouted to the man on the moon.

CHAPTER TEN

Tit For Tat

Early July 1819

"**W**HAT DO YE mean, ye're no' ready to marry?" Brigid stood up from the chess set, both hands on her hips, her feet planted in a wide challenging stance. "Ye can barely keep yer hands off her. How long can ye last? Or do ye plan on taking advantage of my friend?"

Brodie ground his teeth at the last statement. If she were a man or not his sister... "Take advantage? I love Kirsty. Let us enjoy the summer." He sighed and ran a hand through his hair. "For the love of saints, I'm the youngest son. There's no hurry to push me into the parson's trap."

"Ye're teasing her like she's a trout in the stream."

"I've courted her for barely over a month." His jaw twitched. The little chit had nerve. "I *will* ask her sooner or later, in my own time. I'll no' be browbeaten by my wee sister."

"Ye've been together since ye were bairns," his sister argued, her blue eyes flashing.

"Ye both need to stop." Glynnis interrupted the siblings from her chair near the hearth. She set down her needlework with a sigh.

"Brodie, ye wait too long and ye'll lose her. It doesna take a brilliant mind to figure that out. And we'll no' be sympathetic when ye come crying to us."

Brigid sneered. "See?"

"And ye should be minding yer own romantic endeavors." Glynnis narrowed her eyes at her daughter. "Ye run around the glen like my youngest son, scaring away any potential suitors with yer boyish ways."

"But I—"

"She has no idea how to be *feminine*," Brodie jumped in. Good. They'd turn the table on the little minx. "Name one household skill ye have an aptitude for." He crossed his arms over his chest, daring her to deny it.

"I can…" Brigid's foot tapped on one the rag rugs scattered across the floor. Her face brightened. "I can order supplies."

"When I give ye the list," pointed out Glynnis.

"I'll strike a bargain." An idea began to form in Brodie's head. "Prove to us ye have a womanly side by spending a week in the kitchen."

"Saints and sinners. What would I do there?" Brigid's eyes were wide, the apparent horror eliciting a chuckle from her mother.

"Cook." Glynnis nodded. "Yes, a week in the kitchen to learn how to cook. Perhaps Lissie will help so Enid doesna die of apoplexy the first day."

"Help with what?" asked the female in question as she entered the room.

Lissie found solace in the kitchen. After Ian had left last week, Lissie made a dozen loaves of bread and enough biscuits to feed the village. Working the dough seemed to ease her mind, but Brodie had heard more pounding than kneading.

"I've made a deal with Brigid to spend a week in the kitchen." His sister's eyes burned a hole in the center of his forehead. "Yer company might ensure both she and Enid survive the ordeal."

Lissie pressed her lips together and concentrated on smoothing a lock of her umber hair that had fallen over her shoulder. "Enid barely tolerates *me* in the kitchen. I stay out of her way and dinna cause any extra work for her. What if I teach ye how to sew?"

"I'd rather be trampled by a thousand angry sows."

Brodie snorted.

"Perhaps that's how ye could help," said Glynnis. "Ye can help instruct Brigid in some simple dishes, show her some basic cooking skills, and keep her out of Enid's way."

Lissie shook her head. "When I prayed for a distraction after Ian left, this wasna what I had in mind. But I'm happy to help."

Brigid scowled. "What part of chaining me to a stove translates into a wager? What are the stakes?"

Brodie rubbed his chin then grinned. "If ye stay in the kitchen a week, *and* dinna kill any of us, I'll buy ye that sweet little mare ye liked in Dunderave." As an afterthought he added, "If ye actually learn to cook a meal, I'll throw in a new saddle and bridle."

"And if I fail?"

"No more talk of my marriage and ye stay out of my and Kirsty's business." He spread his legs and matched her stance, his chin jutting out in a perfect imitation of his sister.

The challenge had been issued. Brodie recognized the competitive gleam and silently cursed. Her stake would be much higher.

"I agree to the first." She gave him a let's-see-if-he's-paying-attention look. "Can we change the second part of my win?" she asked.

"*Hmmph!* Overly confident, I think." He couldn't read her expression but didn't trust the request. "Depends."

She shook her head. "Aye or nay."

"Fine, what would ye like instead of a saddle?" He had a feeling this would cost him dearly.

"If I learn to cook a dish, ye stop lallygagging and ask Kirsty to marry ye." She sat back down, a smug smile turning up her mouth.

The room was silent. Then Glynnis and Lissie laughed. A soft chuckle at first, then guffaws. The more Brodie scowled, the louder they became with Brigid joining in.

"Ye consider yerself clever, eh?" He glowered at his sister.

"She is clever. She outwitted ye, son. Now accept it like a gentleman." His mother stifled her giggles and nodded her head. "And ye've both made me verra happy."

"But we're wagering against each other!" exclaimed Brigid.

"Aye. Regardless of the outcome, my daughter learns something about running a household. And if she's successful, my son will soon have a wife." She returned her attention to her needlework with a satisfied sigh. "Shall we start tomorrow?"

⟫⟩⟩⟩✳⟨⟨⟨⟪

"I DINNA REMEMBER spectators as part of the bargain," grumbled Brigid with a glare at both brother and grandfather. She leaned against a long plank table, the shelves behind her filled with bowls, jars of spices, and pots. "It's difficult enough in this hot tomb without extra bodies adding to the heat."

Bunches of herbs hung from darkened beams in the low ceiling. The aroma of dried sage and yeast tickled Brodie's nostrils. He sucked in a deep breath. The smells and sounds of this room always stirred fond childhood memories.

Enid growled from her corner of the kitchen. "The inside of a barn full of beasties isna my idea of heaven, either. And since I didna invite ye, I'll ask ye to keep yer opinion of my domain to yerself."

"Saints and sinners." Colin chuckled. "I had to see it with my own eyes. I assumed Brodie was telling me a clanker when he said ye were helping in the kitchen."

"Where's Lissie?" asked Brigid, while she and Enid gave each other

93

a wary glance.

Brodie held back the mirth that tickled his throat. The two women sized one another up, like two billy goats encountering each other on a narrow mountain path. Would they butt heads and fall over the cliff or compromise? "Her mother had a minor accident. Can't use her wrist, so Lissie went to stay with them for a bit."

The look of panic on his sister's face sent both men into laughter. Enid straightened the rumpled apron over her ample form and tucked her frizzy ginger curls under her kertch.

"Out! Or I'll sentence ye both to death by starvation," exclaimed the cook in a tone that had the men scurrying out. The wooden spoon gripped in her fist stressed her point. "I'm only part of yer sibling wager because yer mother asked me. Now, I have work to do, or no one will be eating this day."

Brodie paused in the dark hall, his back against the cool stone, and his head angled toward the door. Eavesdropping was not a usual pastime for him, but this would be a tale retold for years to come. He felt it in his bones.

"First, I'll introduce ye to the weapons of my trade," Enid began. "Knives are sharpened daily. And we'll test the first on Brodie's ear because I ken he's just beyond the door listening to our every word."

For the love of saints, the woman was a witch. "I'm leaving," he called as he bolted up the narrow stone stairs.

Later that day, Brodie tried not to wince as he scraped the top layer of a biscuit with his teeth. Hard as a frozen loch in the middle of winter. His mother and grandmother had warned both men that negative comments would not be allowed. If they couldn't say something pleasant, they were to remain silent. A punishment for both grandfather and grandson.

Brigid watched, a hesitant smile on her face. She was nervous. Brodie tried to remember the last time his sister had not been completely confident. His heart twisted as he gripped the rock in his hand and swallowed. This could be painful. He'd left the edge soaking in his plate of broth, so he'd been able to scrape off a bite without breaking a tooth. Calum had noticed and nodded in approval, doing the same.

"What's the verdict?" asked Brigid. She must have mistaken the thankful gleam in her grandfather's eye for praise. "Enid says it's much better than she expected for my first attempt."

"And what did she ex—" Calum clamped his mouth shut at a glare from Peigi.

"The color seems just about right," Brodie ventured and received a grateful smile from his mother. "What will ye make next?" He would find some reason to be detained.

"Tomorrow I'll attempt white pudding, which should be easy enough. What could be so difficult, mixing together some oatmeal, suet, and meat?" She shrugged. "On Sunday, we shall make a meal in honor of Grandda."

Calum choked on his ale. Brodie bit his lip, the taste of blood holding back his mirth.

"Venison collops," she announced proudly, "and I'll use a recipe from Enid's family that uses red wine."

"Ye'll no' be observing the first time—while Enid prepares it?" asked Calum, his face pale at the idea of a much-loved meal defiled forever. His look cast daggers at his grandson.

"Now why would I do that? I've always learned better by doing a task. It's the mistakes that teach ye the most. That's what the Mac-Naughton always told me when I was a girl." She kissed the top of her grandfather's head. "Since there are no bodies on the flagstone writhing from my first attempt, I'll be on my way. I've work to do in the pasture." Brigid made her escape, her footsteps fading away.

Brodie avoided Calum's glower and appealed to Peigi. His grandmother's lips were pressed together, but he caught the glint of humor in her green eyes before she studied her plate. The merrymaking played havoc in his throat and threatened to erupt. For the love of saints, his lip hurt.

"In my defense, Ma supported this wager." It was a feeble apology, he knew.

"Ye thought it was amusing up until now," Glynnis pointed out. "We all need to make sacrifices for the family."

"Fine," groused Calum. "I hope shortbread is on the menu for Monday."

Both Peigi and Glynnis were known for their love of the sweet treat.

"No reason to be a *crabbit*." Peigi gave him a tight smile at the mention of shortbread. She poked at the golden-baked stone on her plate. "Think of poor Ian, on his way back to Glasgow without Lissie."

Calum snorted. "What of poor Lachlan? He arrives next week and expects Enid's meals after a month away."

"Let's give the rest of these, um, these..." Glynnis's brows drew together.

"Petrified dumplings?" offered Brodie.

Glynnis wagged a hand in the air. "Just give them to the hounds."

Brownie and Black Angus each caught a biscuit mid-air. They settled down, the hard treat between paws, and gnawed at it like a bone.

"Weel, someone finds it tasty," Brodie observed.

"Aye, it's no' a waste, then." Calum pointed at his grandson, his tone imperious. "Ye will be here for *every* meal. No excuses, no emergencies. Or I'll make ye eat what's left when ye come home. Cold."

Brodie grinned. "Ye're right. I canna make my family suffer alone when it's my fault."

"I, for one, am thankful Brodie came up with the idea. Did ye see the earnest look in her eye? She was worried," confessed Glynnis. "My daughter rarely worries about anything."

"Except losing," argued Brodie. His mother hadn't seen the smirk on the pixie's face when she skipped out of the room. He might have underestimated his opponent.

⇥⟫⟪⇤

KIRSTINE HEARD BROWNIE'S howl before she saw Brigid. Charlie began a low whine, his tail thumping furiously. "We have visitors, eh?" She opened the door to let him run ahead.

The deerhounds wrestled in the yard as Brigid waved from the lane. Kirstine watched her hike up the light wool skirt and jog the rest of the way.

"I hope I'm no' interrupting anything." She followed Kirstine into the house. "I've run out of the salve ye gave me for Twiddle. The goat with a gash on his back leg."

"Let me see if I have some ready or if I need to make more. Would ye like some tea?"

Brigid nodded.

She put the kettle on and inspected the pantry at the back of the kitchen. Pulling down a brown crock, she took off the lid. "Ye can have what's left, and I'll send more with Brodie when I finish the next batch."

"If he's still talking to me."

"Because he's angry with ye or because ye've poisoned him?" Kirstine had listened to an entire hour of Brodie's moaning. She was certain he'd be the next martyr of Scotland.

"He's told ye of our bargain, then?"

"Aye. If ye last a week without Enid skelping ye or killing off yer family, Brodie will buy the mare ye've been hankering for. Sounds like he didna think that one through." Kirstine's eyes narrowed as a revelation came to her. "Brigid MacNaughton can do whatever she sets her mind to, but she can't master a stove after almost a week?"

"Have ye seen Lachlan?" Brigid asked, evading the question. "He's different, distracted."

"He may have a lot on his mind."

"I believe it's female." She grinned. "He daydreams, then jerks into consciousness, and turns red as a rooster's comb. As if he was embarrassed at his own thoughts."

"I ken how he feels." Kirstine blushed. "Brodie is in my head night and day."

"Are ye ready to be betrothed?" Brigid's tone implied she had a secret.

"When yer brother's ready. I've had a braw summer so far." The smile on her friend's face was almost triumphant. "Is there something ye want to tell me?"

Brigid shook her head, scarlet tresses flashing. "I'm just in the mood for a *cèilidh*, that's all. And I ken sometimes my brother needs a wee push."

Kirstine sucked in a breath, a rare anger flaring in her chest. "If he needs a push, then I dinna want the proposal. Do ye understand?"

"I didna mean anything by it." Brigid sighed. "Aye, I promise no' to interfere anymore."

"Anymo—"

"Did Brodie tell ye about the venison collops?"

Kirstine shook her head. "I've no' seen him today."

It seemed there had been some confusion between red wine meant for the gravy and red vinegar Enid had set aside for cleaning. By the time Brigid had discovered the mix-up, the platter of collops had been served. Brigid arrived in the dining room as Calum dipped a medallion of venison into the dark gravy and waved it at her. She tried to warn him, but it had been too late.

The fork hadn't left her grandfather's mouth before his eyes almost popped out. Choking and spluttering ensued, followed by cries of concern from her grandmother and mother. When Calum held up his palms to hold off the females and indicate he was fine, Brodie had taken a bite. The chaos began again.

"So a bit of vinegar caused such an uproar?"

"Weel, I also added double of what was needed."

"Tell me that was an accident."

Brigid nodded and placed her hand on her heart. "I swear I misread the recipe. I would never have ruined *Grandda's* favorite meal."

"At least the hounds are getting some fine scraps."

"Och, no' even the beasties would touch it. A terrible waste of good meat," she admitted cheerfully. "Now, I'm off to doctor a goat."

Kirstine considered Brigid's demeanor as she watched the duo disappear over a hill. Her hand absently scratched behind Charlie's ears. "What's her secret, eh?"

Had Brodie confided in his sister? Was he gathering his courage? Her heart pounded at the image of Brodie on one knee, asking her to be his forever. She clutched her stomach to stop the wings suddenly in flight. Her mother's words came back to her.

If he hasna made his intentions clear by the end of the summer, ye need to put him behind ye.

But he would. Brigid wanted to reassure her, hint that all would end well. She threw her hands in the air and spun around, yelling to the charred beams overhead.

"For the love of saints and Brodie MacNaughton!"

Her dream was coming true.

CHAPTER ELEVEN
Teasing, Taunts, and Troths

Late July 1819

BRODIE GAVE HIMSELF a mental pat on the back and rolled to his side, watching the dawn break through his open chamber window. He'd made good progress in their courtship. When he paid attention, he realized how easily he could take over a conversation. He didn't mean to, but something Kirstine said would remind him of an event or opinion, and he'd share it. Lately, he'd ask her a question and bite the inside of his tongue to remind himself to let her speak. His reward had been a treasure of information.

Kirsty's favorite color was blue, like his eyes. She loved any kind of berry, but especially the early strawberries of June. When she wore her everyday clothes, her manner was matter-of-fact. The Kirsty he'd always known. When she dressed in her London fashions, her attitude was saucier. Flirtatious. In her role as healer, he'd seen her tend to an old woman's fever and set the broken arm of a rambunctious village lad. Her manner had been gentle yet firm, efficiency mixed with compassion. He marveled at the many facets of this childhood friend who had grown into such an accomplished woman.

Yet her kisses were always the same, regardless of her attire or mood or task at hand.

Kirsty's plump lips smiled at him from behind his lids. Last night had been particularly heated. Under the moon, his plaid spread over the soft meadow grass, he'd come close to losing control. She'd been so soft, so willing, so *his*.

He rolled back flat, again, and chuckled at the tented bedsheet. If just the image of her pliant body affected him this way, he would lose his mind when they finally bedded.

Each time they were together, he discovered some new tidbit or a nuance in her tone he hadn't heard before. He had come to love her in an entirely different way, feelings that were strange and wonderful at the same time. The vague yearning, for *what* he'd never been quite sure, had vanished. Passion and a joyful anticipation now filled that empty corner of his heart. It was a heady feeling, this being in love. It blended well with his natural exuberance.

After three months, he had no desire to look at another woman. The sight of Kirsty walking toward him across a meadow, or gazing up at him with those chocolate orbs, still made his pulse race and his member stiffen with desire. Instead of dampening, his need grew. Every day. The possibility of losing her sent him into a panic. Another man touching her made him berserk.

Thump! Thump!

"Are ye awake? The day is wasting, ye bumblehead. I have a pony waiting for me in Dunderave."

"Aye, ye blethering female. I'll be down shortly."

BRIGID CHATTERED THE entire ride to Dunderave, riding behind Lachlan so she could ride her new purchase home. Brodie took mental note of where herds of sheep and cattle grazed. They stopped at a stream to let the horses drink and take a brief respite. It was a favorite watering hole for the family when they visited the village. A picturesque dell surrounded by lush pasture and a backdrop of snow-capped gray and green mountains dotted with pine.

It was a braw day, the sun glinting silver on the rushing water. They dismounted and Brigid promptly peeled off her shoes and stockings. Lachlan laughed as she wiggled her toes in the creek's grassy edge. Brodie offered salted beef to his siblings, but Lachlan was still full from breakfast and his sister was too excited to eat. Instead, she wandered onto the moss-covered stones that dotted the brook and dipped her toes in the cool water.

"Careful," called Lachlan. "I'll no' have a sopping rider behind me. If ye fall, ye'll ride with yer crabbit brother."

"I'm in a fine temper," argued Brodie.

"Not after ye pay for that pony."

Brigid snorted, slipped, and caught her balance with both arms spread wide. Her striped pale-yellow skirt dragged across the stone, the hem wet and stained green. She reached behind her and wrapped her copper curls in a knot, fanning her neck.

"It's warmer than I thought," she said. "I'll go barefoot until we get closer to the village."

"Heathen," teased Lachlan.

"Harlot," added Brodie.

They reached the village by early afternoon. Dry stone buildings and thatched cottages lined the main street. At one end was a blacksmith and small dry goods and specialty store, at the other was the *kirk* where Reverend Robertson held Sunday services.

They made their way to the store, stopping at certain points to say hello, or goodbye in Lachlan's case. The owner of the dry goods shop came out to meet them and grinned at Brigid as she slid off the horse without assistance.

"She's all ready for ye. My boy has her coat sparkling like the midnight sky with a full moon." He held out his hand, his shirt sleeve rolled up over a powerful forearm, and shook Lachlan's and then Brodie's. With two fingers to his mouth, he gave a piercing whistle. A high-pitched neigh answered from the back of the building.

"Oooh," moaned Brigid, balancing her weight on one then the other foot.

"Contain yerself, sweet sister," Brodie said with a chuckle, "here she comes."

He had to admit the horse was a beauty. Glossy black except for a twist of white on the forehead, its mane and tail fluttered in the light breeze as it pranced on the end of the rope. Like most Highland ponies, the mare was short but sturdy with muscled hindquarters, a sleek neck, and kind, intelligent eyes.

Brigid approached slowly, murmuring softly in Gaelic, and the animal calmed. She took the rope and continued her soothing words, rubbing its soft nose. "Just so ye ken, I'd have spent a month in the kitchen with Enid for this beastie."

"So she says after the fact," said Lachlan. The humor faded from his face as something caught his attention over Brodie's shoulder.

Brodie turned to see who was behind him. Ross Craigg with his daughter, Nessie. When the girl caught their look, Craigg reached up and pulled the small hairs at the back of her neck. She cringed and eased her head back to avoid the pain.

A knot formed in Brodie's stomach. His fist clenched and un-clenched as he fought for control. With a quick glance at his brother, he saw Lachlan fighting for the same control.

"If ye even glance their way, lass, ye'll pay for it," Craigg warned his daughter, loud enough for the MacNaughtons to hear. "Ye'll associate with fold when I tell ye, or I'll lock ye up until ye're too old to care."

"He's lucky I'll be in Glasgow the rest of the summer," muttered Lachlan, a vein popping out in his neck.

"That's right, ye traitorous cur," called Craigg. "Go to the Highlands and kiss those Lowlander and English arses."

Brodie seized his brother's arm as Lachlan lunged toward the man. "It's no' worth it. He's baiting ye like a bear."

Lachlan growled. "But it would feel so good to have his jaw crunch under my fist."

"The lass will be the one to pay the price. Dinna give him a reason to take his anger out on Nessie." Brodie knew Ross Craig didn't have the courage to plant a facer on another man, who would return the favor in kind. He'd soothe his ego by reminding his women how much strength his punch had.

"That's why ye need to be the next chief. Ye think ahead of the consequences before ye act." Lachlan smacked his fist against his other palm. "I, on the other hand, act and then kick my own backside."

"Shall we go? I want to see how she gallops." Brigid's disgusted gaze burned a hole in Craigg's retreating back. "The mon will get what he deserves some day."

"I hope I'm around to watch," Lachlan griped.

"Let's change the subject for the ride home. Ye still need to tell us about the accountant," hinted Brodie.

"I said there's nothing to discuss." Lachlan turned his scowl on Brodie.

"When a mon insists there's nothing to talk about, it usually means there's plenty he's *not* saying."

⋙✷⋘

ROSS CRAIG COILED a lock of dark hair around his finger and twisted his thumb and knuckle. He chuckled when Nessie's thin neck jerked backward. "I saw ye gawking at them, the lust in yer eyes."

She shook her head frantically. "I only glanced over when they spoke to us."

"First ye embarrass me on Beltane, disappearing into the woods like a common trollop. Then ye run off with that piece of cow dung, and MacDunn has to bring ye back. I expect the eejit wanted me to thank him for the return of my ungrateful daughter." He grunted, a mirthless cackle.

Ross bristled at the memory of MacDunn pounding at his door just before dawn. He'd never had a clue the little wench had planned to elope. It had taken both men to drag the hysterical girl inside, kicking and screaming. The disgust in MacDunn's eyes had cheered Ross.

"Ye see what I put up with? The ungrateful whore." But when he turned to his neighbor, hand outstretched in a rare show of thanks, he realized the antipathy was not aimed at his daughter.

"Ye'll no' blame me for this, Craigg," MacDunn had said and turned his back on the goodwill gesture. "If I'd no' given my word to Calum, she'd be my daughter by tomorrow." Giving Nessie a pathetic look of apology, he had stormed from the cottage.

There would be little chance of a repeat adventure. Nessie had been put on a short lead after that. If she was to be a bedwarmer, it would be a man of his own choosing. One who could improve his standing, make him financially solvent.

"I'd find ye no matter how far ye ran," Craigg reminded the girl now as they came to the edge of town. "Did ye truly think ye'd make it to Gretna Green?"

Nessie shook her head and climbed onto the wagon, eyes focused on the road in front of her. Her face had gone pale. He snapped the reins and the old gelding pitched forward, head down and neck bowed as it slowly pulled the heavy wagon forward. Then he added the whip for good measure. It eased the anger burning in his chest.

"I can walk, Da. We have a heavy load today." She turned to jump down, but he caught a handful of hair and yanked her back.

"Do ye need another reminder of who is in charge?"

She shook her head again, frightened eyes darting at his face and quickly away. Her arms wrapped around her belly, then quickly fell back to her side, and gripped the bench.

Craigg studied her. "Ye're no' hiding anything from me, are ye, daughter?" He softened his tone, running his knuckles gently over her cheek. "I dinna like surprises."

Nessie kept her eyes on the pony. "No, Da, no surprises."

"If ye ever try to leave again without my permission, I'll kill ye. Ye're my property, and I'll do with ye what I want. And if ye do have one in the basket, it'll no' survive long." The tightness eased as he badgered the chit. "No bairn of those sniveling MacDunns will live under my roof."

A tear fell down Nessie's cheek. He reached over, caught it with his thumb, and put it to his tongue. "Revenge is mighty tasty," he whispered in her ear. "Time will tell if ye're lying to me, lass. Time will tell."

⊱⟫⟩⟩✧⟨⟨⟪⊰

BRODIE HAD DONE his best on the ride home, but Lachlan remained tightlipped about the lovely English accountant in Glasgow. A sign it was serious. Their mother hadn't fared any better and would barrage Ian with questions when he arrived.

"How long will the swap be this time?" asked Glynnis. The family had gathered in the sitting room for an intimate farewell. Lachlan would leave in the morning for Glasgow, and Ian would return to the Highlands until a trusted manager was found for the textile mill. "Will Ian stay two months as he did before?"

Lissie's head jerked up at the question. She stood at the hearth and studied the framed miniature portraits of family lining the mantel. Her finger traced Ian's painted likeness. Brodie's heart ached for her, being separated from her husband for such long periods of time.

Lachlan shrugged. "Ian mentioned a trip to Manchester before coming home. He wants to purchase more power looms. Should put him here after the middle of August, I'd say."

"He rubs elbows with reformers and pushes for better wages and working conditions," said Lissie quietly. "I'm afraid for him. The English parliament has little patience for radicals."

"It's about having a voice in Parliament. The Sassenach sit in London and decide our fate while we have no say." Glynnis kept her eyes on her needlework. "Until the working class have a vote, the struggle will continue."

"It's a wee more complicated than that. When the lords *do* compromise with the merchant class, the factory owners neglect to share the profit. They refuse to increase wages or shorten the workday." Lachlan shook his head. "Our mill is one of the few that pay our employees a fair wage. And we still get agitators on our dock, trying to stir unrest."

"In the end, it will be the poor that take the brunt of any political agitation," added Brodie. "But I worry for Ian too. He's the gentle soul of our family but the champion of the undefended. He'll no' back down from a skirmish, especially if he's passionate about the cause."

"Send Colin with him to England," suggested Brigid, curled up on the floor next to Brownie.

Glynnis nodded. "If anyone can keep him safe, it's my colossal cousin."

Colin also worked at MacNaughton Textile. The man was like a stone wall in a storm—heavily muscled, well over six feet tall, and immovable. Even Calum appeared average size when standing next to him. Colin was the kind of man Brodie would want at his back in a fight or on his team for tug-of-war.

"That's no' a bad idea. I heard the orator Henry Hunt will be in Manchester next month. He draws a big crowd." Brodie agreed with the ideology of the rallies but knew how quickly a mob could turn ugly. "The city will be filled with reformers, some with their own agenda."

They sat in silence for a few moments. Brodie and Lachlan studied the chess board, Glynnis worked on her mending, and Brigid enjoyed a last night with Brownie.

"Do ye have to take yer dog?" she asked. "She'll miss me."

Lachlan laughed. "I'm no' leaving her behind again. Ma said the entire glen could hear her howls when I left her last spring. It's time ye stopped sharing my hound and had yer own."

"It wasna a problem until ye decided to stay in Glasgow half yer days," she pouted.

"I'm firm on this, little sister. My hound goes with me."

Brownie's tail thumped in agreement. She rose and stretched, her scraggly butt in the air, and padded over to Lachlan. He scratched the devoted head on his lap. "I'd say the lass is willing."

"I concede," Brigid said with a snort. "Grandda said I could have one from the next litter, but I'll wait for one of Brownie's pups." She stood and joined her brothers, studying the chess pieces. "When ye're chief, Lachlan, ye'll have to take on a male."

Lachlan grunted in response.

It was a MacNaughton tradition. Every chief had a male deer-hound named Black Angus. It had begun during the '45 revolt. Calum's great-great-grandfather had owned a black and gray deer-hound. It resembled the faery dog, Cù-Sìth, a huge dark beast with golden eyes. According to legend, it roamed the moors as a harbinger of death. The unlucky traveler who crossed its path was said to have two weeks to live.

The previous clan chief took advantage of the Highland lore. When the English came too close to the MacNaughton castle, he let loose his canine bodyguard, Black Angus. While no one knew for certain if any Sassenach died, no soldiers made it to the castle.

These days, the dog was more protection against unruly or drunken clan members.

"By the time Ian returns, Brodie should have a date set for his wedding." Brigid smiled sweetly at her brother. "I can prod and push as much as I like, for a bargain is a bargain."

"Aye, but ye still canna make a proper dish," he groused.

"Yet," she quipped. "There was no deadline set, so beware, oh brother mine, I've no' yielded."

"I dinna ken why ye procrastinate," Glynnis said. "Ye love the lass, and she feels the same. Why wait?"

"Because he's a mon with some pride and wants to decide himself when the time is right," Lachlan said in defense of his brother.

"Finally! Someone understands me."

The three women snorted in unison.

CHAPTER TWELVE
Startling Twists and Succulent Turns

Mid-August 1819

K IRSTINE STRETCHED OUT on the plaid and watched the falcon's nest across the small loch. Charlie's ears perked up at the bird's shrill *caw,* and she scratched his neck. Her dark skirt *swished* as her feet jiggled. It was August and still no betrothal. Should she be worried? Her mother made that annoying *tsk* noise each time Kirstine returned from a tryst and shook her head.

"Ye're lost in thought," boomed a voice from above.

She grinned as Brodie settled beside her and motioned for Charlie to move away. The dog moved to a sunny cliff but stayed within sight of the couple. "I'm thinking of my true love and how slow he moves."

"Dinna start haranguing me too."

She flinched at his grumpy tone. "I meant ye're late. And who stepped on yer toe?"

"Brigid." He blew out a loud sigh. "I'm sorry, love. The females in my family badgered me all morning about marriage. I explain—for the hundredth time—it was our business and none of theirs. For the love of saints, we've the rest of the summer."

She chewed on her lip and studied the falcon, sneaking a sideways glance at his handsome profile. "So, another month of courtship?"

"Are ye pressing me too?" His jaw clenched.

He was irritated. Over making a commitment to her. Heat rose up her neck, and she blinked back angry tears. "Never. I'll no' have a mon who doesna want me."

Truth be told, she didn't mind waiting. As long as she knew they would be together. Yet, her heart hurt every time he brushed off the subject. If he loved her, why did he wait? "I've allowed ye to touch in me ways only a husband would," she whispered.

"Och, I've been a perfect gentleman."

"Is that what ye call it?" she huffed. "And I'm harassed just as badly by my mother. She says ye're leading me to the edge of a cliff, and I canna turn back and I canna jump."

The back of his hand stroked her cheek, and she resisted the urge to lean into it.

"Kirsty, I'm sorry," he said softly. "Look at me."

Regret shone in his eyes as he bent to kiss her, his lips soft and persuasive. She opened to him and caught her breath when his tongue tangled with hers. His thumb rubbed a light circle just under her ear lobe, sending sweet, torturous tremors through her limbs. Without thinking, one hand curled around his neck. Kirstine could not refuse him. Her love was pure and her heart obstinate. Still, it galled her that she'd give in so easily.

"I've hurt yer feelings." His breath was hot against her skin. "I'd rather cut off my own hand than hurt ye."

She nodded against his chest. In her soul, she knew this. But her mother's words of caution echoed in her head. A tear escaped. She clamped her lids shut, refusing to let any more leak out. Brodie brushed the lone drop away with a knuckle.

"Marry me, Kirsty. They're right, I just hate being pushed. I love ye with all my soul, and there's no one who would put up with me better."

Breathe! It's the moment ye've been waiting for ye all yer life.

She heard the soft *chink* of his sporran chain as he changed position. He picked up her hand and pressed his lips to her fingers. "Be my wife, Kirsty MacDunn, and keep me honest with yer frankness and a horde of bairns."

When Kirsty opened her eyes, he was on his knees. Sincerity glistened in his sapphire orbs. Her throat grew thick, emotion bubbling up, a tremulous smile curving her lips. *Ye canna cry now, ye ninny,* her brain scolded. *Kiss him and say yes.*

"Aye, Brodie MacNaughton, I'll be yer wife and keep ye honest and give ye a castle full of bairns." She threw her arms around his neck, laughing and crying.

He sat back and pulled her onto his lap. "My heart is lighter already. But dinna tell my mother or sister they ken better than me."

He kissed her on the forehead, then as if he couldn't bear to pull away, he peppered her face with his lips. He pressed her lids close, the tip of her nose, her chin, then claimed her mouth again.

Kirstine's hands explored his hard chest, tracking the ridges of his stomach through his shirt. He sucked in his breath and she smiled against his mouth with her growing power over him. Over the past months, she'd learned what made the vein in his neck pound with desire, how to trace his spine or collarbone lightly with her fingertips.

She was betrothed. She was truly his. The notion made her bold, and she tugged his shirt free from the kilt and touched her palm to his warm, bare skin. She could feel his heartbeat. Her fingers slipped under the band of his kilt, stroked the wiry curls beneath. His manhood stiffened and pushed against her thigh.

"For the love of saints," he rasped, "I'm only a mon. A mon who's been denied for months."

"I'm no' denying ye," she blurted.

In a blink, she was on her back, Brodie feathering kisses down her neck. Kirstine had dreamt of this moment; his tender gaze locked with hers, his mouth and hands strumming her like his favorite instrument. Her breasts were suddenly free, and she gasped as he took one pink tip, then the other, into his mouth. The flame in her belly grew with every swipe of his tongue, his teeth and mouth pulling, teasing the nipples into hard buds.

His palm cupped her mound, and even through the skirt, the pulse between her legs turned into a delicious ache. He pulled the light wool and shift to her thighs, one finger at a time, and slid his hand beneath the layers of material. His stroke was light against her soft inner thighs, and her breath hitched.

When his knuckle rubbed her slick heat, he found her nub and circled it with his thumb. The pounding of her heart reverberated through her core, heat enveloping her body. Her hips rose in answer to this new and intimate touch. A finger, then two, slid into her passage and began a seesaw of back and forth, creating a liquid heat with the sweet friction. Kirstine whimpered, and he kissed her, the sound locked between them. She clutched the plaid under her, fingertips digging into the wool and soft soil beneath while a merciless inferno raged through her. And she wanted more—something more. She locked her gaze with his, the turbulent blue orbs intent but smiling.

He nuzzled her neck. "Should I stop?" he murmured.

Kirstine shook her head.

Brodie's weight shifted to her side, and his lips reclaimed her breasts. He sucked and nipped the swollen tips as his fingers continued their onslaught, slipping in... and out... in... and out of her quivering passage. She moved her hips in rhythm to his thrusts; his thumb caressed her nub in slow, deliberate circles until he coaxed it into a hard pearl.

Kirstine closed her eyes, another husky moan escaping her throat. Her hips jerked up, her breath quick and shallow as his hands and mouth brought her to the edge of heaven. Frustration and pleasure and satisfaction battled within her womanhood, finally coming together as she let out a keening sob. An intense pleasure stirred low in her mons and spread through her like a slow summer storm. It twisted and swelled until she thought she might die from the force of it.

"Brodie," she gasped.

"Let go, love," he whispered in her ear. "Give in to the blaze, let the passion take ye."

Then his mouth was on hers, his tongue traced her lips, and Kirstine surrendered. Let the spiral of heat break into waves of ecstasy that rippled through every corner of her body. Her muscles spasmed around his fingers, and he plunged faster and faster until she arched and cried out his name.

Slowly, the fog lifted. She could hear the chirp of birds again, Brodie breathing, her own panting, and Charlie's soft growl. Kirstine smiled.

"Ye're so beautiful when ye're in the throes of passion," Brodie said, his tone husky as his eyes trailed up and down her body. His thumb moved lightly between her folds, and he smiled at the light tremors still shuddering through her at his touch.

She lay there panting, in a daze, wondering how her legs would ever hold her up again. *Merciful heavens!* Her limbs had grown heavy as tree trunks, and she could easily take a nap. The hound rumbled again. *Shhhh*, she soothed.

The idea came to her that they were not finished. Brodie had not entered her. Kirstine held up her arms. "Come inside me, Brodie."

He shook his head. "I'll no' take yer virginity here under the pines. It will be a proper ravaging in a bed." He eased down next to her, elbow to the ground, head resting on his palm.

"So this was not a ravaging?" She wondered what could possibly be better.

"This was just a taste, love. There's so much more to come." He brushed her cheek with the back of his hand and leaned down to kiss her. "I'm of the opinion we should jump the broom sooner than later."

Kirstine sighed, her fingers still trembling as she pushed a thick lock of midnight hair from his forehead. "Whatever ye say, Brodie."

"Weel, I always said a satiated female is a compliant female."

"I think ye're right." Could she make *his* insides quake? Make him cry out her name? "How do I return the favor?"

"A lesson for another day, my voracious lass." He stood and held out his hand to help her up, tugging her snugly against him. His need was evident and rigid against her belly. If he let go at that moment, she would drop to the ground in a heap.

She slapped his shoulder and wriggled her hips against him. "Voracious?"

He growled at her frisky squirming. "Aye, and I hope it never changes."

"She's fine, Charlie, I dinna hurt her," Brodie called to the deerhound, who responded with a bark. "Next time, perhaps ye should leave him back. It's a wee strange to have a set of eyes on ye when ye're..."

He kissed her soundly and collected the plaid. Kirstine imagined them folding a blanket in their own cottage, laying it across their own bed.

She giggled and sprang up on her tiptoes to kiss him, clutching the soft wool between them. "I love ye, Brodie MacNaughton, more than life itself. Ye've made me the happiest woman in Scotland."

"Och, no' the happiest woman in the world?"

Kirstine rolled her eyes. "Will ye never be satisfied?"

"Aye, lass." He waggled his eyebrows. "I plan on being satisfied soon and verra often."

KIRSTY WILLED HER legs not to run. He'd watch her leave, wait until she disappeared over the next hill. Her heart was close to bursting and she couldn't wait to tell her mother. As soon as she and Charlie were out of sight, she picked up her skirts and flew the rest of the way home.

"He's done it!" She flung open the heavy door. Her mother looked up from the bowl and pestle and paused her work. The scent of lavender filled the room. It helped to calm Kirstine's racing pulse. "I'm betrothed."

She fell into the chair, panting.

"I dinna believe it." Her mother rose to hug her daughter. "The mon does have some sense. Is he off to tell his family?"

Kirstine nodded. "He says he prefers to be wed sooner than later." She blushed at the memory that had caused the statement.

"Judging from the color of yer face, that would be the wisest course." Ma sat again and picked up her pestle. "He's no' had his—"

"No, he's been verra gallant and wants to wait for a proper bed." The heat increased, spreading down her neck.

"That's good to hear, I suppose. Have ye made any other plans?"

"Och, I was so happy, I just wanted to rush home and tell ye."

Her mother seemed pleased by that admission. "I would say three or four weeks would give us enough time for a trip to Glasgow or Edinburgh. We'll need to make ye a new dress for the ceremony and decide what ye will take with ye."

"I'll be living in the castle," she murmured. "I've dreamt about that since I was ten." They both laughed.

"Weel, ye willna dream about it anymore. I'm happy for ye, my sweet. Verra happy for ye." She pushed the bowl and dried lavender toward Kirstine. "Now, while ye're still a poor, unmarried lass, I'll ask for yer help."

With a distracted sigh, Kirstine began crushing the fragrant leaves. Her body still hummed and tingled from Brodie's touch.

This was just a taste, love. There's so much more to come.

Never had she been so eager for the future.

➤➤➤◄◄◄◄

BRODIE TOOK THE narrow, winding steps two at a time. His boots thudded softly on the worn stone as he emerged onto the first landing. Voices drifted from the dining hall and wiped the silly grin from his face before he entered.

His grandparents, mother, and Lissie sat at the long table. All four wore a look of misgiving.

"What's with the long faces? I've no' seen so many unhappy faces since Brigid was in the kitchen." He paused, seeing his grandfather cringe. "No, tell me she's not at it again."

Peigi nodded. "She's determined to make a good dish. It's that competitive nature ye both inherited from yer grandfather."

"Me? Ye've no' played chess with me since ye barely won the last time. Afraid of losing and ye canna tell me any different," huffed Calum, then waved at Brodie. "Sit down and take yer punishment. I hear her coming."

Brigid emerged from the staircase with a tray of tarts. To Brodie's surprise, they were golden brown, several with minced apples oozing from the edges.

"It smells mouth-watering," ventured Glynnis.

"And flaky," added Lissie.

She carefully set down the tray and watched each family member gingerly choose a pastry. Brigid stood between Brodie and Calum, her hands twisting, her teeth gnawing on her lower lip.

Calum sniffed the warm shell and tentatively licked the warm spicy center oozing out. His blue eyes lit up with wonder. "The apples are verra tasty," he exclaimed before sinking his teeth into the crust. "Mmm."

Brodie's eyes widened as his grandfather's closed. He looked at his sister who had begun to smile, hope shining in her eyes. He bit into the dessert and chewed, then took another bite.

"Oh gracious," exclaimed Peigi, "these are wonderful."

His sister beamed. Was that a tear glistening in her eye? Could she be that happy over a tart? Or was it because she had bested her brother? He hated to admit defeat, but the pastry was delicious. He'd gladly have two.

"It's light and buttery," his mother said around a mouthful.

"The outer shell is just the right crispness and the apples are baked to perfection," agreed his grandmother.

Brigid plopped down next to him, beaming. "Brodie?"

He nodded. "Ye've won, little sister."

"Now ye have to ask Kirsty to marry ye," she said.

Brodie was surprised. Not a hint of smugness in her tone. He opened his mouth to announce he'd already done so, when she leaned over and kissed his cheek.

"She's my best friend in the world, and I've helped to make her the happiest woman in the glen." She studied the table and traced the wood grain with a finger, pink staining her cheeks as she admitted, "Kirsty is the sister I've always wanted. That's why I never gave up. Ye've made both our dreams come true."

Brodie studied his sister. She wasn't the sentimental type, and a confession like this would have been difficult for her. Brigid may have a tough outer shell, but she was more fragile on the inside than she would ever admit. How could he belittle her effort by telling her it had been unnecessary? That he had already proposed? He blew out a loud breath, knowing it would be misinterpreted.

"Aye, ye minx. Consider us betrothed." He smiled. "And I'm proud of ye. And Enid, for letting ye back into her kitchen."

"Weel, about that," she said with a grin. "I may no' be so welcome again."

"It seems congratulations are in order for both my grandchildren," boomed Calum. "Fetch the decanter, Brodie. We'll drink to Brigid's accomplishment and Brodie's future betrothal."

A disturbance in the courtyard interrupted their celebration. Lissie looked out the paned glass. "Someone has arrived on horseback. The beastie is sweating as if the devil had chased them."

A muffled yell from below and an answering voice, and soon the panting man stood before them. He held an envelope in their hand.

"Jason, ye've come from the mill?" asked his grandfather.

The man nodded.

"Och, mon, dinna just stand there. What is it?" coaxed Calum in a quiet but firm voice.

But the hairs rose on the back of Brodie's neck. The villager worked for them in Glasgow. There was no good reason he would be racing pell-mell to MacNaughton Castle.

Jason opened his mouth, but no words came out. Brodie saw the pain in the man's brown eyes. Instead, the man walked forward and handed his chief the envelope.

Brodie admired his grandfather's composure as he calmly cracked the seal and opened the letter. As he watched Calum's face, his own heart cracked. Tears sprang to Calum's eyes, and he swallowed once, then twice as he tried to form words. Silently, he handed the paper to Glynnis and Peigi, their heads bent together as they read.

"What?" Brodie couldn't stand it.

Lissie shook her head, her eyes shining. "Ian's coming home, isn't he?"

Calum stood abruptly, his chair tumbling backwards and clattering against the floor. His face turned up to the ceiling, his fists above his head, he let out a heart-wrenching roar. Peigi rushed to his side while Glynnis clung to Lissie. Brigid clutched Brodie's hand, her nails digging into his flesh as she reached for the letter.

Brodie sat in shock, hearing bits and pieces as Brigid's tremulous voice read the news.

"Demonstration... Manchester... Ian killed... Lachlan and Colin bringing him home..."

"Oh, Brodie," cried Brigid.

He turned to his sister, wrapped his arms around her, and prayed this was a bad dream.

CHAPTER THIRTEEN
The Parting Glass

CRACK! KIRSTINE AND her mother both jumped when the door banged against the wall. Her father stood, blocking out the meager light of early dusk. "It's a tragedy," he said in a cracked voice.

A chill snaked down Kirstine's spine, waiting for the rest.

"Ian MacNaughton is dead. Killed at St. Peter's field during a political gathering. Women and children dead too. The newspapers called it a massacre.

"Oh, sweet Jesu!" Her mother's hands flew to her chest, then reached out for Kirstine.

"Ian? Are ye sure?" It couldn't be true. She'd just seen him a month or so ago. "I didna say goodbye when he left. He canna be gone."

"They're having a terrible time at the castle. The news crushed Calum. He clutched at his chest, Enid said, and fell to the floor. It was like a great tree toppling to the ground." Her father beckoned them both. "Fetch yer satchel. Ye're needed. Brodie has sent off messengers to inform the chieftains, and I've been tasked with collecting both of ye."

"Brodie," Kirstine gasped. "My poor Brodie."

"He's standing strong, Kirsty. Took over as if he'd always been chief, giving orders and seeing to the women." He cleared his throat.

"I was proud to do his bidding."

Kirstine swallowed the lump in her throat.

"No time for sentiment, Daughter." The women scrambled into action while Mr. MacDunn came around with the wagon.

"I'll drive," said her mother. "Saddle up yer horse, in case I need ye to fetch something for me." With a steady hand, she cracked the whip, and they rumbled down the lane. "When we arrive, I'll go straight to Calum and Peigi. Ye tend to the younger lasses, give laudanum to Lissie, and then find yer mon. He'll need comforting."

Kirstine nodded. She was used to people scurrying about the grounds, but the place was almost empty.

An eerie quiet hovered over the courtyard. A redheaded stableboy ran up and held the harness. "Are they all inside?" asked Mrs. Mac-Dunn.

He nodded, his mouth trembling. "The MacNaughton, he... the sound that came from the castle made my skin crawl. It was horrible." The boy swiped at his tear-streaked face, then led the horse and wagon away.

The women gazed up at the windows of the round tower. A faint moan carried on the breeze. Her mother gathered her skirts in one hand and gripped the satchel in the other. "Take a deep breath and remember: no crying. We're healers, and we're needed now."

⇒⟫✕⟪⇐

KIRSTINE SHIVERED AS she entered the dim great hall. The evening chill seeped through the open windows and soaked into the cold stone walls. No matter the time of year, evenings in the Highlands had a bite to them. Especially in these old, drafty castles.

The flame from a single lamp lit Brodie's face, lines of exhaustion deepened by the flitting shadows. He'd aged in the last hours; the responsibilities of family and clan weighed heavy on his tired shoulders. Brodie had stood in for Calum, meeting with clan heads to answer questions and accept condolences as the news spread. He hadn't wept yet, according to her father; there'd been no time to grieve.

He was slumped in a wingback chair, swirling an amber liquid with one hand, the other dangling near the floor. He tipped back his head to drain the glass. His rumpled shirt had been pulled from his kilt, which was in disarray and left his knees bare. He was a sorry sight, and Kirstine's eyes burned with her own unshed tears. Sorrow for the loss of a brother, a son, a grandson, a husband, a friend. Ian's death left a massive void in the hearts of his family and clan.

"Do ye care for some company?"

He didn't answer but gave a curt nod.

She knelt in front of the hearth, added peat, and started a small fire. What could she say? Nothing would ease the pain. When she turned to face him, he set his glass on the small table next to him and opened his arms to her. Kirstine settled on his lap and pulled his head to her chest. She rocked back and forth as his grip tightened about her waist. No, she realized, words weren't necessary. He needed her love, her strength. She stroked his hair and held him tight.

His tears were silent at first, soaking her bodice, until he sucked in a shaky breath and released a long, mournful sob. She soothed him, stroking his hair and his back. The peat was only embers when Brodie leaned his head back against the chair.

"What would I do without ye?" he rasped. He scrubbed his face with one hand, the unshaven jaws scratching beneath his palm as he closed his bloodshot eyes. "I keep hoping this is just a night terror. If I go to sleep, I'll wake up to see Ian walk through the door."

"What can I do for ye? Have ye eaten?" She wondered how much he'd drank of the half-empty decanter.

"I'm no' hungry."

"That's no' the question."

He snorted and opened his eyes, the corner of his mouth twitching. "Sweet Mary, how I love ye, Kirsty."

"And I love ye too, but ye'll be no help to Calum if ye drink yer supper." She stood and held out her hands. "Let's go see Enid and get some food in yer belly."

"I'll follow yer lead, love."

Enid had been busy. Her puffy eyes belied the smile she gave them. "It will be a small army in and out, paying their respects over the next week. I thought I'd get started with the food," she told Kirsty as she set a plate of cold fowl, cheese, and fresh bread on the trestle table. "How is the MacNaughton?"

"Doing well and insisting it was no' apoplexy but a bit of dough he choked on." Kirstine remembered his gray pallor when she'd first seen him.

"Ye canna blame a mon after such a shock. Especially at his age," added the cook.

"Dinna let him hear ye say that," said Brodie. He picked at the hunk of cheese.

"And how are ye, lad? I heard ye did a fine job in yer grandfather's stead." Enid squeezed his shoulder. "Calum will be proud."

He nodded. "He'd expect nothing less, and we must all do our part."

Kirstine picked up the conversation. "Aye, his color is already improving. Ma says he should rest a couple days, but she doubts he'll listen."

"Ye'll no' keep Grandda in bed for long. He'll want to be up to meet Ian when…"

Enid and Kirstine shared a concerned glance. "And Lissie?" asked the cook.

"I gave her something to sleep. Brigid and Glynnis are with her. Even in their grief, they're strong and worried about others."

"They're MacNaughtons," Enid agreed.

Kirstine heard a loud *sniff* as the portly woman resumed her work.

"Will ye be leaving soon?" Brodie tucked her hand in his. "Ye must be tired too."

It occurred to her, in that moment, how thoughtful he'd become.

"I believe my mother is giving last-minute instructions to Peigi about now, then she'll check on Brigid and Glynnis once more. Da said he'd let me know when he would bring the wagon up."

"And I'm here to do just that," Mr. MacDunn said behind her. "I'm going now." Brodie stood when the older man held out his hand. "I'm sorry for it, son. We all loved Ian, and he'll be sorely missed."

"Thank ye... for everything," Brodie said hoarsely. "The women's skill... all yer support today, it's greatly appreciated. Yer family is indispensable to this clan."

Her father ducked his head, and Kirstine realized he was embarrassed. Brodie stepped forward, and the two men hugged, thumping each other on the back.

"Whatever ye need, we're here for ye," her father said.

Kirstine watched him leave, pain etched on his weathered face. She tried to swallow the lump in her throat. *Ma told him we're betrothed. He knows we've lost a family member too.*

Brodie touched her arm. "I need some fresh air. Can I walk ye out?"

"I'd like that." She went to Enid, and the two hugged.

"I'll be back tomorrow," she told the cook. "I'm happy to lend a hand."

"Dinna tell her, but I'll miss Lissie poking around." Enid smiled and sniffed again. "She's a help to me, and I've become a wee spoiled."

Brodie took Kirstine's hand and led her from the kitchen. They made their way outside to the back of the castle. They ambled through the herb garden and turned toward the courtyard. He laced his fingers through hers and sucked in a deep breath of the night air. She wanted to hold him and absorb his pain. Instead, she would be his rock, support him in any way she could. Be strong for him when he faltered with the anguish of losing a brother.

Just before they reached the courtyard, he stopped in the shadows and pulled her close. "I'll need to lean on ye to get through this, Kirsty."

His breath ruffled her hair, and she tightened her arms around his waist. She could feel the soft beat of his heart against her cheek. Reaching up, she cupped his face. "I'm here for ye, Brodie. As I always am."

He enfolded her wrists, turned over her hands, and placed a kiss on each palm. Then his lips lingered against hers. A soft, sad, gentle kiss that twisted her heart. "I was the most fortunate of men when I left ye earlier today. How quickly life can change."

She nodded, breathing in his familiar musky scent. How could a day begin with so much hope and end in such misery?

"Did ye tell yer folks about our betrothal?"

She nodded again, chewing on her bottom lip. Regret clouded his blue eyes.

"I didna have time, I'm afraid," he said, his voice hoarse.

"It can wait, Brodie. Now is no' the time to share such joyful news."

He sighed and gave her an apologetic smile, wrapping her close and sinking his face in her hair. "We'll make the announcement in a week or two. When we both decide the time is right. I'm sorry, Kirsty. For the love of saints, I wish—"

"Shhh," she soothed when his voice broke. "I'm here, we're together. We canna ask for more now. Let's be thankful we have each other."

"Ye're right. We need to count our blessings in times like these." He stepped back and laced his fingers through hers, leading her back to the path. "Ye're sure Grandda will recover?"

"Ma thinks he gave his heart a scare, but it wasna a terrible spasm for the pain stayed in his chest. He has a strong beat again and his color is back." Kirstin grimaced. "When James Weir died last year, she remembers his pain spread through his arm. He was weak and barely conscious. She said the foxglove helped for a while. When she listened to Calum's chest, he had a strong beat again and didn't need the tincture. He's a resilient mon."

"He's a stubborn mon," chuckled Brodie.

"I'd be surprised if he was still in bed tomorrow, regardless of what my mother or Peigi orders. We'll have to keep an eye on him. He'll tire more easily for a spell."

Wagon wheels crunched on the courtyard stones. Women's voices floated from the receiving hall, and they could hear Mrs. MacDunn and Glynnis discussing the laudanum. Kirstine wished she could stay but tamped down her anxiety.

"I'll be fine, love," he whispered in her ear as if reading her mind, "but promise ye'll be back tomorrow."

"Nothing could keep me away."

Her father tied his horse to the back of the wagon and helped both women onto the bench. They waved goodbye and rode in silence until they were out of sight of the castle. The tears threatened now that she had a respite from her obligations. Kirstine laid her head on her mother's shoulder. Her eyes began to droop when she remembered.

"Och, did ye mention the betrothal to anyone?" she asked.

They both shook their heads. "Of course no'," her mother said. "It would be improper. Why?"

"Brodie had no time to tell his family before they received the news about Ian." She blinked, her eyes burning again. "We canna announce it now."

"What matters is that he asked, and he loves ye. It's all I ever wanted for ye, Kirsty." Her mother patted Kirstine's cheek. "A few weeks are a wee inconvenience for a lifetime of happiness. It's but a storm cloud that will hover and dissipate."

She nodded as tears streaked down her cheek. And then she was wrapped in a maternal hug, rocked and soothed as she had for Brodie.

"Love and loss have equal parts in the cycle. We learn to embrace one and accept the other. Without the loss, ye dinna appreciate the life."

With a sob, Kirstine let her anguish soak her mother's chest.

"There, there, my sweet lass. It's been a long night, and ye can let it out now. Unburden yerself so ye'll have the strength to do it again tomorrow." She kissed the top of her daughter's head and brushed back the wet strands clinging to her face. "Yer grandmother always said tears cleansed us and helped us to heal what ailed us on the inside."

If that were true, Kirstine thought, they'd need to fill a loch to rinse away the pain and sorrow of the days to come.

One week later

"YE'VE NO' TOLD yer brother about yer gooolden angel?"

They were in the formal parlor where Ian had been placed. It was a large room and easily held a large group paying their respects during the week-long wake. It was Colin's turn to watch over Ian's body. Lachlan and Brodie had joined him in the formal parlor, and they passed the time as most single men did. They'd drank and shared stories of their women, past and present. Brodie tried again to learn about the female who had taken Lachlan's fancy. His brother remained tightlipped.

"I was unconscious and out of my wits, Cousin, after dealing with those agitators on the dock," Lachlan said with gritted teeth. "I might have escaped the knot on my head if ye'd joined us in a timely fashion."

Brodie snorted at the murder in his brother's eyes. This would be a story to remember, if only because Lachlan was so desperate for it not to be told.

"Ye can make all the excuses ye want," Colin said. He slapped Lachlan on the shoulder. "I dinna ken why ye'd keep it quiet. She's a bonny lass."

"I'll keep my mouth shut if ye do the same," warned Lachlan.

Colin laughed. "I have no secrets. I'm a wee infatuated with Miss Rose. She's a companion to the woman Lachlan lusts after."

"I—"

Brodie interrupted his brother. "Wait, let's go back to the angel story."

Mischief twinkled in Colin's blue eyes as he smoothed back his raven hair, then leaned forward with his elbows on his knees. A sign he was warming up for a good tale. "Weel, Lachlan had given one of the chancers on the dock a Glasgow kiss. Had a real goose egg on the back of his head. Sorcha bandaged him up and ordered to him lie down."

Brodie settled into his chair, arms crossed and a huge grin on his face. "Of course, my brother insisted he was fine." Sorcha's brothers had a reputation for pummeling one and another. As the eldest sister of the family, she'd become proficient at mending bones and stitching up gashes. Now a plump middle-aged widow, she'd moved to Glasgow to work in the mill and was the first to be called for any injuries.

"Of course. Sorcha warned him he could get woozy at any time, so he promised to go directly to the office and rest." Colin winked. "The office is where Fenella, er, Miss Franklin works."

"I didna want to leave the mill. Kindly leave out yer opinions and recite the facts." Lachlan scowled at his cousin.

"On his way up the stairs, his head began to spin. One of the lads and Miss Franklin got him to a chair and called for Sorcha. By the saints…" Colin began to laugh, shaking his head as he remembered.

"Go on," urged Brodie, wondering at Lachlan's red neck. "My brother is blushing."

"Miss Franklin began to sponge his face with cool water. Lachlan began mumbling, incoherent at first, but the smile on his face was easy to read. A mon only smiles like that when—"

"Just finish the bloody story before Grandda comes in," grumbled Lachlan.

"So Sorcha is standing in front of Lachlan, and he mumbles 'Come here' and something else we couldna understand. Sorcha leans forward, and..." Colin laughs again, wiping at his eyes. "Lachlan says, 'Come here my gooolden angel,' and reaches his hands out to grab Sorcha's chest."

Brodie let out a bellow. "What did she do?"

"She grinned and told him to remember he's a long time dead and—"

"I didna touch them," spluttered Lachlan. "I collected my wits."

Brodie hugged his stomach as he joined Colin, their guffaws echoing against the walls. Just as they caught their breath, Calum wandered in with a small barrel of ale.

"Sounds like a good story." He sat down next to Brodie.

"For another time, Grandda," pleaded Lachlan. He reached over and took the keg, filling his cup. "This is half empty."

"Aye, right," Calum agreed and turned to Colin. "I'm ready to hear what happened to my grandson that day. Ye're my brother's son and my favorite nephew, so it's best coming from ye than anyone else."

The smiles faded and the big man nodded. "It's no' pretty."

"Death never is," agreed Calum.

Brodie listened to Colin's retelling of the events in Manchester, England. A peaceful congregation of citizens, an almost carnival-like atmosphere with thousands of men, women, and children waving banners. A band played as they waited to hear The Orator speak on the working man's right to vote and fair representation.

The cavalry of mostly local volunteers arrived. Townspeople waved and smiled, assuming they had been ordered to attend in case there was any mischief. But when Henry Hunt began to speak, the cavalry moved their horses into the swarm and drew their sabers. Terror had rippled through the packed mass of bodies. The soldiers had pushed the crowd from several sides, yelling to disperse, as they slashed their way to the platform. With nowhere for the people to escape, it had been a massacre.

Ian and Colin had been in the middle of the throng, next to a woman and her baby. When a horse reared, its hoof kicking the child from its mother's arms, Ian had thrown himself over the bairn. The steed had trampled him before Colin could push his way through the chaos. He had lifted Ian's crumpled body over his head and plowed through the pandemonium. Brodie knew his cousin blamed himself. But his brother had been a grown man with his mind. No one was at fault except the cowardly mayor who had ordered the assault.

After Colin had finished, they had sat in silence, each man wrapped in his own thoughts. Then Calum had opened a bottle of Ian's favorite scotch. One memory led to another, and soon they were laughing and remembering how Ian had lived rather than how he died.

"If there's another world, he lives in bliss. If there is none, he made the best of this," crooned Lachlan, his cup held high.

Brodie stood, wobbling, but his feet planted firmly on the ground. He was certain of it, but he squinted at his shoes to make sure. Satisfied, he added, "To Ian!"

"To Ian!" echoed Colin, towering above them.

"Bring it down here, Cousin. If I try to reach ye, I could land on my arse," slurred Lachlan.

They raised their mugs, Colin lowered his, and they clanked, ale splashing over the sides. Calum looked at the spots that now speckled the Axminster carpet. "If Peigi sees that, we're all dead men. And I'll no' take the blame."

"If Peigi sees ye with a drink in yer hand, *ye're* a dead mon," Colin said with a smirk. "She doesna believe ye choked on a wee piece of meat."

"It's time for a tune." Calum changed the subject. "Shall we keep with tradition?"

"Strings or pipes?" asked Brodie. He and Lachlan both played the fiddle, but his brother had the better voice.

Colin ran a hand through his black hair, smoothed his wrinkled shirt, and wiped droplets of ale from his dark kilt. "I'd be honored to play." He proceeded to the corner of the room where he'd left his pipes the previous evening. "Brodie?" He held up the violin.

"Aye." Brodie smiled at his mother and grandmother as they entered the room.

"Ye're just in time," declared Calum, swinging his arm and the mug of ale behind his back.

"I think I'm a wee late." Peigi inspected the state of her husband.

"Ye've a suspicious mind, *mo chridhe*."

"Ye're a sloppy sneak," she said, her eyes fixed behind Calum.

Brodie followed her gaze and saw the splashes of ale mysteriously falling from his grandfather's back. He also recognized the gleam in his grandmother's eye. She wouldn't scold her husband this day.

"We were about to sing 'The Parting Glass'. Ye'll no' ask me to toast to Ian without a wee swallow." He gave her his most charming smile. "Will ye?"

"The Parting Glass" was a time-honored song at many funerals and always ended in a mandatory toast of whatever the dearly departed would have preferred. The first time Brodie heard it was at a great-uncle's funeral when he'd been only six. It had been his first taste of whisky.

"Shall we join them?" Glynnis asked Peigi.

"They may need us to remember the words in their condition."

Lachlan poured six tumblers of Ian's favorite scotch and arched an eyebrow at his mother.

"Lissie is sleeping, and Brigid is in the stable."

"No, I'm no', and yes, I'll partake," Brigid announced as she came to stand by her mother.

Colin readied himself in front of the hearth. He adjusted the drone and tested the chanter with several practice blows. Taking in a deep breath, he filled the bags, and the first keening notes pierced the room. Brodie positioned the fiddle under his chin and laid the bow to the strings.

Lachlan began the song, his voice deep and resonant. The familiar lyrics combined with his brother's deep, resonant voice brought a smile to his face and tears to his eyes. He joined the next chorus.

So fill to me the parting glass
And drink a health whate'er befalls
Then gently rise and softly call
Good night and joy to you all

Of all the comrades that e'er I had
They're sorry for my going away
And all the sweethearts that e'er I had
They'd wish me one more day to stay

Calum added his rich tenor and everyone but Colin sang along to the bittersweet melody.

But since it fell into my lot
That I should rise and you should not
I'll gently rise and softly call
Good night and joy to you all

Fill to me the parting glass
And drink a health whate'er befalls
Then gently rise and softly call

Good night and joy to you all

Brodie's arm fell to his side, the bow sharp against his bare knee. The haunting notes of the pipes faded, and Colin set the instrument down. The misty-eyed group gave one another watery smiles and held up their glasses. "To Ian."

CHAPTER FOURTEEN
A Bungled Betrothal

Early September

"I T'S TIME TO tell my family." Brodie and Kirstine were in the pines, listening to the rush of the waterfall below. He wondered if they would still come here once they were married. "My aunt and cousin are coming from England. I want to make the announcement before they arrive."

"Are ye sure?" Kirstine asked.

Brodie brushed a silky red lock from her cheek and replaced it with his lips. His self-control was waning. They lay beneath the pines in their usual spot. His finger made a lazy trail from her chin to the hollow of her throat. With a flick of his thumb, he pulled the tie of her shirt loose, then again and again.

"Ye've been more than patient." He breathed in the sweet scent of heather that lingered in her hair. The bodice fell away, and he easily pulled on the shift to free her breasts. A groan scratched at his throat. "For the love of saints, I need to get ye to the kirk." The ache in his crotch was painful, and it wasn't happening just when he was with her. Every morning, he woke with a raw throbbing, his dreams of her soft curves still lingering in the early dawn light.

"How is yer—"

Kirstine gasped as his mouth covered her nipple. He blew on it lightly and watched the pink bud pebble. His hand slid down her belly and under her skirt, his palm tickling the thick curls of her mound, his fingers parting her soft womanly petals. Bloody hell, she was hot and wet and inviting. He wanted to take her and the devil with a bed.

"Brodie, let me love ye."

The huskiness of her tone spurred him on. He nipped and teased her other nipple to a point and slid his fingers inside her. Her hips rose to meet his thrusts, and she whimpered in anticipation. His thumb lightly rubbed her nub, then he bent his head and flicked it with his tongue.

"What... oh God, oh Brodie!" She cried out as he sucked and licked at the delicate pearl, swollen and hard with his ministrations. Her body shuddered; her nails dug into his shoulders.

Brodie eased himself next to her, withdrawing from her passage and kissing her mouth. He continued sliding his fingers between the sensitive flesh, wet from her spent desire, until her panting eased. "Ye're so lovely when ye're satisfied."

She smiled, eyes closed. "Will a bed change my body's reaction to ye?"

He laughed. "No, but it will ease my conscience."

Kirstine rolled over to her side and leaned her head on her fist, the other hand pulling his shirt from his kilt. "It's my turn."

"Och, no, love. I—" Her slender fingers crept under his belt, shyly touching his member. He covered her hand with his and moved it in a slow circle. Just for a moment, he'd indulge her. Allow himself a brief instant of pleasure after weeks of restraint. And then he was lost.

His thoughts scattered as her palm brushed over his sensitive tip. He stiffened; the pulsing forced his eyes closed, and his head fell back as he moaned her name. She chuckled softly and continued to lightly rub the head while his hips moved with her.

"There'll be consequences if ye dinna stop," he said through gritted teeth but blew out a frustrated sigh when she obeyed.

Kirstine chuckled softly and loosened his belt. Her hand gripped his shaft, sliding up and down in a slow rhythmic motion, mimicking the way he'd caressed her. His body betrayed him, refused to listen to his brain and stop her. As Brodie gave in to the passion, her timid movements became bolder, firmer; the swirl of pleasure in his belly churned into a squall of desire. When his manhood swelled, he thrust up into her grasp, hungry for fulfillment. Her strokes quickened with the first drops of his seed, sliding up and down his shaft until he let out a long, satisfying roar that echoed against the cliffs across the loch. His body shuddered as he struggled for breath, the climax leaving him weak and dazed.

"I hope no one is nearby. Ye could wake the dead with that shout." Kirstine giggled. Her warm breath tickled his ear.

Without opening his eyes, he pulled her close. She snuggled against his chest, her head tucked under his chin.

"That shout has been building for months. I couldna have been quiet if my life depended on it." He ran a hand down her hips and cupped her bottom. "I think I need a wee nap."

Kirstine laughed and held up her hand, wiggling her fingers. "So much power in such a small appendage."

"Aye," he said, grabbing her wrist, "and it's brought down mightier men than me."

Two weeks later

KIRSTINE STUDIED THE pastry then gave her friend a dubious look. "Ye're sure it's safe?" Brigid had stopped by on her way to the MacDougals. Glynnis was now cooking for the two Liams and had sent her daughter with a basket.

Brigid laughed. "I've no intention of eliminating my newfound sister. It's the second time I've made them properly. So ye're no' an experiment."

She bit into the flaky crust, and the sweet berry filling coated her tongue. "It's good," she admitted. "But ye won yer wager with Brodie, why are ye back in the kitchen? Did yer mother sprinkle ye with faery dust while ye slept?"

"Verra funny. My Aunt Maeve and cousin Gideon are arriving tomorrow, so I thought I'd try again."

Kirstine raised a doubtful eyebrow.

Brigid let out a long dramatic breath. "I heard Ma talking last night. She wants to send me to Aunt Maeve's in England for the next *Season,* as if we dinna have seasons here."

"Och, she means the marriage Season." She took another nibble. "Merciful heavens, I canna imagine ye in London. From what I've read, it's all proper conversation and remembering when to curtsy and who is a mister or lord or lady and such-and-such."

"Aye, so I ventured into the kitchen again *and* plan on flirting with MacDougal at the cèilidh. I hope it will be enough to change her mind. Ye'll be there?"

"Of course. Yer aunt hasna been home since she wed. I look forward to meeting her and yer cousin. Does Liam ken of yer plans of seduction? Ye may want to warn him. Or pick someone younger if ye're to appear sincere." Kirstine worried for her friend. She might have appeared tough and boyish on the outside, but inside, Brigid wanted love as much as the next woman.

"When I find the right mon, I'll ken it here." Brigid patted her chest. "So far, he has no' been in my line of vision."

"So ye believe in love at first?" asked Kirstine. This was a new side to her old friend.

"I accept that it's possible. Ye've loved Brodie since ye could remember. My mother and aunt both fell in love at the first meeting."

Brigid stood and brushed the crumbs from her skirt. "The problem is, I've already met everyone in the glen and Dunderave. And not even a flutter in my belly when I met MacDougal."

"Perhaps a trip over the border would be good for ye. Consider it an adventure."

Brigid snorted. "I've had enough adventure battling with Enid in the kitchen. But it was worth it. It got me the sister I've longed for."

Kirstine hugged Brigid at the door. "I thought ye won a pony?"

"Aye, for lasting a week in the dungeon. But for mastering a dish, I—" Brigid's eyes grew wide, and she collected her basket from the table. "My, where did the day go? I must be off."

Suspicion clenched at Kirstine's stomach. She grabbed her friend's sleeve and held firm. "Brigid MacNaughton, ye'll no' leave until ye explain yerself."

"Weel," she hedged, suddenly interested in a loose thread on her skirt. "I was truthful about the wager. At least the part I told ye about. It's the portion I omitted."

"And?"

"Weel, if I lost, I promised no' to pester him about proposing, and I heeded yer request and kept my goading to a minimum."

"I appreciate that," Kirstine agreed drily. "What about the pastry?"

"Brodie added to the original bet and offered me a new saddle and bridle to go with the pony if I managed a *tasty* dish. When I wanted to substitute for something else, he agreed, assuming it was a different purchase." Brigid scuffed the toe of her boat against the wood planks. "If I succeeded, he had to propose—sooner than later. And he did."

The two women glared at each other.

"And I dinna care if ye're upset because ye both love each other, and I have a sister now." Brigid stuck her chin out and collected the basket.

"Dinna count yer sisters before their wed," Kirstine yelled after the retreating form. "He hasna got me to the kirk steps yet."

She clenched her fists and growled, which sent Charlie into a bout of howls. Scratching his ears, she wondered what to do with this new information. How could Brodie have kept this from her? Had he really proposed only because he'd lost a wager?

Don't be silly, her mind argued. No, she didn't doubt his love. She did doubt his humility, though. The arrogant oaf. He had some explaining to do, and she would enjoy watching him squirm while he did so. Brigid wasn't sure which was worse: Brodie's wager or Brigid's smugness that she was responsible for their betrothal.

⟫⟩⟨⟨⟪

BRODIE WAS WAITING for her at their usual place and time. She smiled sweetly and accepted his kiss. When he tried to pull her close, she ducked under his arm.

"We need to talk, Brodie." Kirstine stood on the plaid, afraid to sit down or let him too close. His touch always muddled her brain.

"About?"

"Wagers and ponies and betrothals."

His face fell, those blue eyes avoiding her gaze. "Ye've been speaking with Brigid."

She nodded. "How could ye? Is our love so trivial that ye'd bargain with it?"

"It wasna like that." He tried to take her hand, but she clasped her fingers tightly behind her back. "A mon needs to make such decisions on his own and no' be harangued under his own roof. I was only trying to gain some peace for a bit. Ye ken how much I love ye."

His voice was low and convincing; her reserve was crumbling.

"I remember ye complaining about it. It's the other half of the bargain that has my feathers ruffled." She stepped off the plaid, putting more distance between them. "Brigid feels *she's* the reason ye finally asked me."

140

Anger flared in his eyes. "Ye truly think Brigid could push me into something so serious and final?"

Kirstine shrugged as the knot grew in her stomach. Maybe she was making too much of this. "She certainly believes it."

"Ye dinna understand," he said, his tone cajoling again. "I went home that day, and she'd made some tarts. The expression on her face was so pitiful, I couldna tell her, right then, that I was already betrothed. I wanted her to enjoy her moment."

Kirstine softened and ventured a look at Brodie. He was so handsome today. His black hair combed back, a fresh shirt already untied at the throat, showing a hint of his chest.

"Will ye set Brigid straight?"

He nodded, stepped forward and pulled her close. "Aye, as soon as I get home. I would have told her later that day, but we got word about Ian." A shadow flashed over his face. "After that, it didna seem important. Until now." He nuzzled her neck.

"I want us both to be ready when we join hands." She tipped her head back and gave him access to her neck, her pulse quickening. Would his effect on her ever dampen?

"To be honest, I'd decided to wait until the fall." His lips trailed fire along her shoulder.

"What changed yer mind?" He pulled her hips closer and squeezed her buttocks, sending sparks of heat to her core. She closed her eyes and moved against him.

"When we met that day, I saw the tears in yer eyes and ken I'd hurt yer feelings." One hand came up to cup her breast, kneading and teasing through her bodice. "I felt sorry for—"

Her eyes flew open. "What?"

His hands came away, palms out as if to defend himself. "Och, let me rephrase that."

"Ye felt sorry for me?" Kirstine planted her fists on her hips and blinked back angry tears. Oh, how she wanted to skelp the man.

"Ye looked so pitiful. The tears… and trying to be brave. I just wanted to make ye happy."

Without thought, her hand came up and slapped his face. Her palm stung; his eyes flashed shock, then ire as he rubbed his cheek.

"I'll no' accept a proposal out of pity. There are plenty of men who would be happy to take me as a wife and mother of their children." Her voice wavered, and she whistled for Charlie. "Consider yerself free."

"Wait, Kirsty. We need to settle this."

"Brodie, I've waited a lifetime for ye." She shook her head, needing to get away, to run as far and as fast as she could. "I accepted the selfishness and understood yer reluctance to marry before yer eldest brother. But I have my pride, too, Brodie MacNaughton. Save yer benevolence for a female who's happy to settle for it."

"There's a dozen I could call on right now." He folded his arms across his chest.

She whistled for Charlie, and turned to leave, refusing to let Brodie see her tears.

"If ye think so poorly of me, I wonder why ye wanted to marry me at all," he growled, still rubbing the imprint of her hand on his face.

"Because I love ye, faults and all," she whispered. "And I assumed ye felt the same."

"Dinna walk away, then want to make up later." He yelled as she followed her hound down the hill. "I'll no' be here moping for ye."

What just happened? Kirstine had never planned on breaking off the betrothal. She'd only wanted Brodie to admit to his part in the sibling rivalry and apologize. Her temper had gotten the better of her. It wasn't like her to spout off like Brigid. Kirstine had always been calm in the face of conflict or during an emergency, and yet, he'd set her off so easily. Why? Perhaps her trust in Brodie was fragile when it came to his affections? Or maybe she was tired of always being so understanding.

His comment about feeling sorry for her had hit a nerve, and the slap had been spontaneous. It had taken them both aback. Now it was too late, too late to take back the hurtful words, too late for apologies. Brodie was stubborn. It would be a long while before he'd listen to any explanation she cared to give, and his ego would never allow him to apologize. Oh, if only he would.

As soon as she was out of sight, Kirstine picked up her skirts and ran across the meadow, away from Brodie, away from her lost dreams. If only she could have left her broken heart in the pines.

➤➤➤✦◀◀◀

"WOMEN ARE THE most irritating, confusing, pain-in-the-arse creatures the Good Lord ever put on this earth." Brodie paced up and down the dining room. Glynnis sat quietly, her needle poking through the linen as the thread silently moved through to the other side.

"What did ye do, son?"

He stopped and turned on his heel, agitation churning in his gut. "Why does everyone always assume *I'm* at fault?" He began pacing again. "She believes I'm arrogant and selfish."

"Aye, right."

"Ye're my mother. Could ye show me a wee sympathy here? I've just lost my bride."

"Ye ken where to find her." His mother never looked up from her sewing.

Calum sauntered in. "Sounds like there's heart trouble here, and it's no' mine." He thumped his chest. "Strong as ever, I am."

"Grandda, tell Ma this isna my fault."

"I canna do it." He walked to a side table and poured a short glass of whisky and held up it up, a brow arched his bright blue eyes.

"Aye, might as well," Brodie groused. "Any words of wisdom ye'd care to impart?"

Calum snorted. "My wife wasna willing at first either. She left me a letter, freeing me from our betrothal."

Brodie plunked down on a chair beside his grandfather. "I never kent that."

"I had to go after her. On Hogmanay, no less." He tossed back the whiskey and ran a hand through his gray-streaked raven hair. "Another wee swallow?"

Brodie finished his own and slammed down the glass for a second drink. "How did ye convince her?"

"Made it easier to agree than to keep saying no."

"I'll no' make a fool of myself, chasing after a fickle woman." He scowled at his mother's bent head, and the smirk she didn't try to hide.

"Look who's calling someone fickle," she murmured.

His grandfather chuckled. "This has nothing to do with pride. It's about proving yer unswerving loyalty and having the mettle to do whatever it takes to make matters right. It's about being the kind of mon the clan would someday accept for their chief. A leader with an unshakeable foundation who looks to hearth and home. Ye canna understand a mon's need to protect his wife and children if ye dinna have any yerself." Calum stood and stretched, letting out a loud yawn. "But mayhap ye and Lachlan have changed yer minds about that plan."

Brodie opened his mouth to argue but caught his mother's eye. "What?"

"He's right. We all ken ye love her. That's the easy part of commitment." Glynnis sighed and put down her needlework. "She's stood by ye, and put up with yer selfish ways, since ye were both children. She's loved ye and waited for ye to become the man we all kent ye could be. And in yer gratitude, ye'll let yer pride get in the way of a lifetime of happiness."

His gut twisted. They were right. They were all right. The wager had been childish. Brodie had only recently realized what had been under his nose all the time. A future without Kirsty wasn't a possibility.

"What should I do?" he asked. "I've made a mess of it, I'm afraid."

"Ye do just what yer grandda said. Ye wear her down with thoughtfulness and court her until she canna stand it any longer. Make it easier for her to say yes than to keep turning ye down." Glynnis smiled and leaned over to pat his cheek. "Things have always been too easy for ye."

"What if she willna give me the chance?" Had he gone too far? The game of Spillikins came to mind. Was this the one stick that sent pile toppling?

"She loves ye, son. Just put a little effort into it, let her ken she's worth it."

CHAPTER FIFTEEN
Sorry Is As Sorry Does

The next day

KIRSTINE'S MOUTH DROPPED open. "Mrs. MacNaughton, ye're the last person I would expect at my door."

Glynnis smiled. "May I come in?"

"Of course." She stepped aside. The older woman swept in, her gold-pinstriped, umber skirt swishing against the doorframe. Her auburn hair was swept up in a tidy bun, and the MacNaughton blue eyes held sympathy. Not pity. There was a difference.

"I assume ye've heard?" Kirstine asked, chewing on her bottom lip. "Can I get ye some tea?"

Glynnis nodded and sat down at the kitchen table. "Is yer mother here?"

"I am," answered Mrs. MacDunn from the back of the cottage. She emerged, tucking a stray brown strand under her kertch, a basket over her arm. "Have ye come for the oils, then?"

"Aye, it's one reason."

"And the other?"

"I'd like to speak with Kirstine," admitted Glynnis. "And ye're welcome to listen and advise."

"I'll put the kettle on."

Kirstine tamped down her nerves and forced her hands to lie still in her lap. "I hear yer sister is visiting?"

Mrs. MacNaughton grinned. "Maeve hasna been home since she married. Her English earl didna care for the Highlands, so we always met at the textile mill in Glasgow. It's the first time my nephew, Gideon, has seen the castle. Scotland has been quite an adjustment for him." She reached out and caught Kirstine's hand. "Now, we need to talk about my numpty-headed son."

To Kirstine's surprise, her mother took neither side. "Sounds as if they backed each other into a corner and couldna find a way out."

"But Brodie loves ye and will be asking yer forgiveness," added Glynnis.

Kirstine's heart leapt. Could they mend this rift? The argument had escalated so quickly. She'd gone over it a hundred times in her mind since yesterday.

"... And I'm here to be certain ye make him work for it."

Her mind snapped back at those words. "How?"

"He'll be wooing ye, and ye need to keep him at arm's length. No kissing or namby-pamby. Let him yearn for ye. And when he asks ye to marry him again, tell him ye're no' quite ready. Perhaps the next time he asks."

Kirstine bit her lip, her mouth quirking up at the corner. "That will tug at his temper."

"I hope so. A mon should appreciate his wife, and my son has taken too much for granted in his easy life."

"And ye're sure he'll ask again?"

"As the moon rises every night." Glynnis patted Kirstine's knee. "We'll see all of ye at the cèilidh in two weeks? Maeve and Gideon have given us a grand excuse for a distraction."

"We'll be there," answered Kirstine's mother. "In fact, I suspect my daughter will be in a new dress. One of those fancy London styles."

⫸⫷

Late September

"YE'RE OFF TO Dunderave?" asked Brodie. "Do ye need me?"

"Ye have work to do," Calum said with a wink. "Besides, it's a social visit. Yer Aunt Maeve hasna seen the villagers in decades, and she wants to introduce Gideon. I'll extend a personal invitation for the celebration next week."

"My poor cousin will be surrounded with well-wishers. I tried to talk Gideon into wearing a kilt, but he'd have none of it." Brodie laughed. "We'll continue the onslaught, though."

"How goes the courting?"

Brodie's smile faded. "She's pleasant enough but distant. If I could just kiss her, it would save time."

"I dinna remember ye being in any hurry before."

"Which is why I'm in this predicament now."

After the family left, he cut some wood for Enid and exercised two of the young colts. Later in the afternoon, he began his daily mating ritual, as Grandda called it. He took a half-bath, shaved, and dressed in a clean shirt and his Sunday kilt, added fresh stockings with bright flashes to the sides. Then he saddled a horse and headed to the meadow to collect a posy for Kirsty.

A week of this ridiculous routine and he hadn't even had a kiss for his effort. Kirsty had returned to her role of dear friend, but his body wasn't accepting the change. Yesterday, they had sat together at the swimming loch, and he leaned down to kiss her. She had turned her head, and his lips grazed her cheek. He'd held his breath to stop the groan and wondered if he'd seen pity in her eyes. *Pity!* If Brodie didn't know better, he'd swear she was enjoying his discomfort. But what really got his goat was she and Brigid were thick as thieves again.

Speak of the devil. Both women were in the yard singing, bent over a squat barrel, stirring the contents with two poles. Kirsty's backside swayed back and forth as she moved the pole, and his kilt formed an instant tent. *Like a hound on a scent, ye traitor,* he thought, looking down at his lap.

A mental image of the old Widow Weir, naked, tamped down his desire as he quietly dismounted. He pulled a stale oatcake from his saddlebag and *clucked* to Charlie before he threw the treat. The dog bounded down the land, so Brodie was free to sneak up on the sweet bottom beckoning him across the yard. The girls paid no mind as they belted out their tune. That Rabbie Burns could write of love as well as any female.

And fare thee weel, my only luve,
And fare thee weel a while,
And I will come again, my luve,
Tho' twere ten thousand mile!

Just as Brodie reached the pair, his hand pulled back for a wee randy slap, and Brigid turned.

"Saints and sinners!" she screeched, dropping her pole and clutching her chest. "Ye're as quiet as a ghost."

Kirsty turned, eyes narrowed at his arm frozen in mid-swing. "What were ye planning on doing?"

Blasted sister. "I was told ye were going to Dunderave with the rest of them," asked Brodie. He could hear the irritation in his voice and gritted his teeth when Brigid gave him a smug smile.

"I'm helping Kirsty dye some cloth. Ma said there was no need for me to tag along and complain the entire day."

"Weel, I can take over for ye." Brodie peered into the dark liquid, then held up the flowers. "For my bonny lass."

Brigid rolled her eyes. "Ye can do better than that with Grandda's blood running through yer veins."

"Did I ask yer opinion?"

"Did we ask for yer company?"

"I trust this to be one benefit of *not* having siblings," interrupted Kirsty. She leaned her stick against the barrel and wiped her hands on her apron. "They're lovely, Brodie. Thank ye." She turned to his sister. "And thank ye for yer help, Brigid. I think we're about done for now."

A silent message seemed to pass between the women, for Brigid opened her mouth then shut it with a nod. As she walked past him, Brodie reached out and yanked an auburn curl. It was childish, he knew, but his nerves were on edge, and she was grating every one.

Brigid whirled and pushed back at his chest. It caught him off balance and time seemed to slow. His body teetered, arms swinging in giant circles as he fought to stay on his feet. Then he lost the battle and splashed backside into the tub of dye. The women scattered to avoid the indigo spray, laughter trailing behind them. He gritted his teeth and gripped the rim of the barrel as his feet dangled over the edge.

"*Brigid!*"

His bellow echoed down the glen as Kirstine's eyes grew wide. Her hand covered her mouth, but it didn't silence the giggles. Brigid pressed her lips together and attempted a straight face. Then the two friends looked at each other and burst into another round of guffaws, clutching at their bellies.

Brodie heaved himself up. The blue water sluiced down his legs and soaked the back of his white stockings. His elbows were a deep indigo, and he didn't want to know what his cheeks looked like. He cast his most ferocious glare at Brigid.

"Uh-oh." His sister turned on her heel and ran down the lane, almost falling over Charlie on his way back. "I'll see ye tomorrow night, Kirsty," she called over her shoulder.

"Ye'll no' see the morning if I catch ye," he yelled after her, waving the posy he still clutched in his fist.

Kirsty made a valiant effort to stop giggling, but obviously, his appearance was too comical. He held out the mangled flowers. She accepted them and led him toward the well.

"We'll need to clean ye up quickly or the dye will set. We'll rinse off the worst of it, then I'll fetch some lye soap."

The first bucket washed away any remaining arrogance.

The second cooled his temper.

The third made him realize how ridiculous he looked—clothes drenched, skin splotched purplish-blue—and sent Charlie into a fit of howls.

"Come up to the house now and bring two pails of water." She patted his cheek and gave him a sweet smile. "I'll see how much color I can scrub from yer arms. It's mostly around yer elbows." Her eyes traveled down his body.

"What about my legs?"

"Aye, I'll do what I can within, but I'm not reaching up yer kilt. Ye'll have to deal with your buttocks on yer own."

"I remember a time ye had no qualms with touching me beneath my kilt."

Pink spread across her face, and Brodie wanted to kiss her. Those laughing, brown eyes, the full lips... he bent his head just as she turned and hurried to the cottage. He sighed. This had gone on long enough. There would be a proposal today.

Kirsty carried a chair outside. "Take off yer shirt and stockings off and sit down. I'll no' have a mess inside."

He obeyed as she bent over the pail and lathered the soap on a brush. He studied the rounded bottom that had started this ordeal. A smile curved his lips. Brodie had never been one to sulk, and his natural humor finally won out. When she swung to face him, her eyes landed on his chest.

He grinned. "I suppose ye can thank Brigid for the view."

Her eyes shot up to his face, gazes locked. Kirsty broke first. The giggles bubbled out again, mixing with his laughter and several snorts.

She picked up his arm and began to scrub. "I apologize for the roughness, but dye isna easy to remove."

"Aye, right." He felt as if he'd just crawled through a field of thistles. By the time she finished his arms, his skin was raw and pink but only a light layer of blue remained. He stood on the chair, and she did the same for the back of his calves and a halfway up his thighs. The discomfort was worth the intimate contact. Kirsty touched him again, her hand skimming along his skin as it followed the soft bristles. Maybe he wouldn't skelp his sister after all.

"It's as far as I go," she said, dropping the brush in the dark soapy water. She dipped the ladle in the second bucket and poured it down his legs. "I'll give ye some oil to soothe yer skin. It should also help to fade more of the color."

She returned with a small bottle and a soft cloth. "Hold out yer arms." She gently applied the oil over his chafed skin, then turned his body around and squatted behind him.

Brodie's jaw clenched as the oil smoothed over his lower thigh and calf. "For the love of saints, Kirsty. How much restraint do ye expect a mon to have?"

"Dinna blame me for yer randy actions. Ye did this to yerself." She sounded just as frustrated.

He looked over his shoulder. Her hand slid a little farther up his leg, and he heard her breath catch. She stood quickly and pushed the bottle of oil into his hand. "Apply more when this soaks into yer skin. With any luck, it will be gone in time for the cèilidh."

Her hand lingered in his, and he pulled her against him, heedless of the wet wool of his kilt. "Marry me. Let's be done with this charade."

Kirsty hesitated then looked him in the eye. He thought he saw regret, and it tightened the knot in his stomach. "I'm no' quite ready. Perhaps the next time ye ask." And she ran into the house, Charlie on her heels.

Brodie stood there barefoot, his mouth open. *Not quite ready?*

Those words didn't sound like Kirsty. In fact, the response had sounded almost... practiced.

"Maybe there'll be no next time," he yelled at the closed door, yanking on his stockings. He tucked the oil in his sporran and collected his horse. Something smelled foul, and it wasn't the dye. Time to have a talk with the MacNaughton women.

Dunderave

THE DAY HAD started so brightly. Ross Craigg replayed the afternoon in his head, trying to figure where, precisely, his plan had gone wrong. The entire MacNaughton family was visiting the village today, even the MacNaughton's Sassenach-loving daughter. What was her name? Maeve. If he remembered correctly, she'd had eyes for Rory MacDunn as a lass. Shaming MacDunn in front of her would have made his fall from grace that much sweeter. But now it was all falling apart.

Ross brought his sheep into Dunderave, deposited them behind Reverend Robertson's cottage, then explained to the minister there had been foul play.

The reverend hadn't wanted to bother the chief.

"MacDunn stole my sheep, altered the lug marks to make them look like his own, and ye dinna want to bother the mon?" He'd spat at the ground. "It's his responsibility to settle this dispute. MacDunn should be on his way. I'll wait behind yer house with the beasties."

"The sheep could have easily wandered into yer flock. It's happened before," Reverend Robertson disagreed. "But if it will end yer complaint, we'll have the MacNaughton decide."

Calum had arrived with two mangy hounds and his English nephew. Ross had rolled his eyes as the reverend explained the basics of sheep farming to the eejit welp.

"We use common pasture and have two ways to identify the

sheep. Keeling—a paint on their wool—distinguishes from a distance who owns the sheep or lug marks can be cut into their ears. Each farmer has his own particular notch."

"Mine is one V, and MacDunn's mark is two overlapping Vs." Ross had wanted to get on with it.

Calum had inspected the animals and frowned. "It's no mystery to me. They all have the MacDunn lug marks."

"The second mark was added." Ross had enjoyed the worry on his MacDunn's face. "Look closer, ye'll see one of the Vs is more recent."

Calum had rubbed one ewe's ear, his eyes narrowed. "MacDunn, what kind of thievery is this? Do ye think my brain's no bigger than this sheep?"

"I swear to ye by all that's holy, I didna add that mark," the accused had bellowed, panic in his voice.

Craigg had been careful to keep the smile from his face, tasting revenge. It was one thing to argue over livestock that had been mixed together. It was another to steal. If the marks had been added, it was proof of deceit. Men had been hanged for such an offense. The best-case scenario was flogging. Either way, Craigg would have won. Until the English pup interfered.

"You're saying you never tampered with those ewes, and no one under your employ touched them to add a mark?" the mealy-mouthed grandson asked.

MacDunn shook his head.

"He's a liar! He did it, and he'll hang for it, by God."

But Calum had played Almighty. "I make the judgments here. We are in Scotland, not England. I'll no' hang a man for a bit of wool, but I'll flog him myself if he's lying."

"The MacDunns have a reputation for pilfering. Ye'd take his word over mine? My cousin Alisabeth lives under yer roof, and ye side with this common criminal?" Craigg had sneered. "Or are ye getting weak in yer old age and afraid the MacDunns will retaliate?"

"I take offense on both counts, Craigg. Our clans have been at peace for too long for ye to speak such filth."

Craigg had seen the warning signs of MacNaughton's temper. He'd decided not to risk a huge fist in his face. Then the reverend, MacNaughton, and the Sassenach had gone back into the cottage to confer. Craigg had stayed behind, guarded by Calum's black hairy beast. The Death Dog. And in ten minutes, his plan had gone awry. He and MacDunn were ordered to return with their children.

Now, he gave Nessie a sideways glance as they stopped in front of the minister's house. "Someone will pay for this," he muttered at her bent head. "And keep that shawl pulled tight, ye hear me?"

She nodded and pulled the length of material around her belly.

"Keep yer mouth shut and let me speak for both of us."

They pushed their way into Reverend Robertson's small crowded parlor. Nessie kept her head lowered as he'd instructed, her dark hair hiding her face. MacDunn and his skinny boy were already there. Craigg heard the end of the conversation. *Damnation!* The MacNaughton knew Nessie had tried to elope with the MacDunn boy.

Calum looked at the tall, lean lad. "Hamish, how old are ye?"

"Seventeen, sir."

"Do ye love the lass?"

Hamish gave Nessie a sideways glance and nodded. "With my last breath."

"Weel, let's hope it doesna come to that. Nessie, do ye love him?"

"She's too young to ken what she wants," groused Craigg.

"I'll hear the lass's own words, Ross," Calum ordered.

Nessie sniffed, picked up the edge of her voluminous apron, and wiped at the tears trickling down her cheeks. "With all my heart and soul."

Stupid bitch! Craigg let out a low growl and knocked her on the side of her head. She stumbled, and Hamish lunged for him. *The foulsome cur.* Craigg stepped back, digging his nails into his daughter's arm. Both deerhounds jumped to their feet with a snarl, teeth bared and hackles up. MacDunn wrapped his son in a bear hug, the boy kicking and throwing punches in the air.

"Touch the lass again, Craigg, and ye'll have my fist in yer face. Ye understand?" Calum said in his kingly tone.

He grunted in reply, still scowling at his daughter for ignoring his order of silence.

Calum smiled at Nessie. "Lass, are ye with child?"

One hand rubbed the side of her head where her father had smacked her. Now the other hand instinctively cradled her belly, showing a swell under the ample material as she nodded.

"Shut yer feckin' mouth, ye no good whore!" Ross warned.

Nessie shoved a fist in her mouth to stifle a sob.

"Weel, this isna so complicated after all, is it?" Calum crossed his arms over his chest and grinned. "Craigg, it seems ye have two choices. Ye give yer daughter consent to marry the lad so the bairn has a father, and I don't flog ye. Or I flog ye, and tell the whole village what's conspired here."

"Ye'll not tell me what to—"

"Make yer choice."

With gritted teeth, Ross spit out, "Marry the little brogan off. She's dead to me."

"Fine," said Calum in a cheery voice. "And as dowry, she'll bring along anything her ma would have given her. As a wedding gift, ye'll give them the sheep in the back, seeing they already have MacDunn's lug mark. Agreed?"

"Aye," Ross growled.

"Aye," agreed MacDunn as cheerfully as the chief.

"Rory MacDunn, will ye take the lass in? They canna live with the Craiggs."

"Aye." He gave a sharp elbow to his son. "See what comes from trusting the chief? Justice."

"And a lovely wife," added the minister.

"And there'll be no laying of hands on the lass before she leaves yer home. Do we have an understanding?" Calum's eyes locked on Ross.

Craigg jerked his head in assent but looked directly at Gideon, his eyes blazing with hate. That no-good Englishman had somehow been responsible for this. He felt it in his bones. "I dinna ken why this is any of yer affair or how ye were privy to my business. But it's not over yet."

"Mind yerself, Ross. Ye're lucky the MacNaughton is a generous man," the minister said grimly. "Dinna put more strife upon yerself or yer family. Let it go."

Calum smiled at the young couple. "We came with an invitation to MacNaughton Castle, a cèilidh to celebrate the return of my daughter, Maeve. We may as well as have a wedding while we're at it."

Craigg drove home alone. He didn't care where his daughter slept for the next week. It was war now. Another marriage decided by the great MacNaughtons. When he first discovered Nessie was pregnant, he'd wanted to beat her until she lost the babe. Then today's scheme had come to him. After he'd revealed MacDunn as a thief, Ross would have smothered the bairn at birth and dumped the bastard on MacDunn's doorstep.

Instead, MacNaughton had demanded an *apology* and the five sheep with MacDunn's lug mark. The animals were worth more than the sniveling girl. He drank deeply from his flask.

His father's words haunted him, wouldn't stop ringing in his ears.

Dinna follow them like the rest of the bleatin' sheep. Keep yer own counsel and bide yer time.

It *had* been his time. He clenched his fists; he would call in some help. It would cost him, but a hired man would also be the perfect scapegoat if anything went awry. Another plan began to form. The wedding would be at the castle. Everyone drunk and off their guard. Behind the castle gardens was a copse. Nice and dark.

Craigg slammed open his cottage door and shouted for his wife. She was huddled in bed, pretending to be sleep. He grabbed her long braid and jerked her head up, backhanding her. "Get up! I'm hungry." Her whimpers eased his anger.

By God, they would all pay.

CHAPTER SIXTEEN
Untimely Impediments

A week later
MacNaughton Castle

KIRSTINE TWIRLED AROUND her bed, imagining a dance with Brodie later that night. She smoothed out the indigo dress with a silvery gossamer overlay. The waist was high, and the neckline was low. Too low, in her father's opinion. A delicate lace trim, matching the sheer material, had taken her a better part of a day to sew.

"Are ye ready?" Her mother stood below. "We need to leave in an hour."

"Aye. I'm so happy for Nessie and Hamish. He's marrying his true love, and she's escaping the devil."

"That mon will get his comeuppance. Beasts like that always do, eventually."

Kirstine pulled on her most expensive stockings and secured them with leather ties. The soft leather shoes were snug but comfortable on her feet. She climbed down the ladder and handed Ma the ribbon. Turning, she lifted her long tresses so her mother could tie the ribbon about her waist.

"Get my ivory comb and mirror and sit down at the table." Her tresses were soon arranged, fastened at her crown with another thinner, iridescent ribbon, curls dangling on the back of her neck. Her mother added sprigs of dry heather and stepped back.

"Pretty enough to be getting married yerself."

Kirstine picked up the small mirror and turned her head one way, then another. Her stomach tumbled at the reflection. Was that really her?

"How many times has the lad proposed?"

With a smile, Kirstine counted out loud. "The dye disaster," she began, giggling at their nickname for that day, "and the last three days in a row."

Despite his threats, Brodie had returned to propose every day. She gave him the same answer each time. "I'm no' quite ready. Perhaps the next time ye ask."

He'd smiled and nodded, as if he were in on the scheme. "A treasure is worth waiting for," he'd responded each time.

"And ye've stood firm?" her mother asked.

"Aye, but tonight I will tell him yes. I canna play with his heart any longer." Kirstine knew he was sincere, and it was time to move on with their lives. The butterflies in her stomach fluttered again as she thought of his lips on hers, his hands skimming along her—

"Did ye hear me?" asked Ma. "Never mind, I ken where yer mind is. Now, here comes yer father with the wagon. Remember yer shawl."

Kirstine fetched the tartan wrap, checks of forest green against a deep blue that matched her gown. She wasn't in a hurry, since Brodie wouldn't attend the wedding. Brigid had sent a message that she and Brodie would be late. A cow in distress, a fall birthing, took priority over a cèilidh. Brodie had volunteered to help. She smiled and wondered if he considered it voluntary. His sister had a way of pressing her unwilling brothers into service.

MacNaughton Castle bustled with activity. In the main hall, Peigi gave last minute orders to housemaids and cooks. "Be certain there is plenty of wine and ale. My husband willna be happy if we run out of either. Once the food is served, ye may join in the festivities. Keep at least two on duty throughout the day and evening to check the pitchers and platters."

Guests already filled the hall for the late morning ceremony. Tables lined one wall with small pies, breads, and fruit compotes. More trestles were set up with benches for eating and visiting, white linen spread across the wooden boards with candles and crystal water bowls for washing. Glynnis and Lissie were overseeing the table decorations, placing entwined circles of marzipan at intervals on the table. The sugar creation sparkled and shed twinkling crumbs along the length of the linen. On the dais, silver goblets and plates had been set out for the guests of honor and their hosts.

The smells were as dizzying as the surroundings. Venison and pig sizzled on spits, and scents of simmering dishes floated up from the kitchen. Nessie and Hamish had hoped for an elopement at best. Fate, and the MacNaughtons, had given them a memorable ceremony and the best gift of all. A chance to be happy. What they made of their lives from here would be up to them.

"Ye're lovelier than the first day of spring after a long winter. If my brother doesna come to his senses, I'll marry ye."

Lachlan stood smiling down at her, handsome in his tartan kilt and blue dress coat, auburn hair combed back, the silver chains of his dress sporran glittering. He had returned for the festivities and would escort the bride to the kirk. Ross Craigg had refused to attend the ceremony. No one had argued his decision and hoped he didn't change his mind.

"Today is about Nessie and Hamish, but I thank ye for the compliment." Kirstine blushed.

A stranger stood at the entrance of the hall dressed in the English fashion, his wine-colored tailcoat fitting snugly across his shoulders with an embroidered gold waistcoat and matching trousers. He had the same dark looks and blue eyes as Calum and Brodie, except his features were sharper, more English, she guessed. His intense gaze searched the room and landed on something behind her.

Kirstine turned to see Lissie blushing, then disappear into the crowd. "Is that yer cousin and aunt?"

"Aye." He waved them over. "I'll introduce ye."

Maeve was a tall, graceful woman with shining auburn hair and a brilliant smile. She resembled a younger Peigi, but with the Mac-Naughton eyes.

"Are ye enjoying yer visit?" Kirstine asked after the introductions.

"Aye, it's been too long." Maeve nodded at several passersby. "I've no' attended a cèilidh since I was a girl. I feel years younger just being here."

"I'm surprised ye've kept yer brogue." There was such a difference between mother and son when they spoke.

"I'm afraid it gets stronger the longer she's here," explained Gideon. "May I ask if you are related to the MacDunns of the day?"

Kristine nodded. "Hamish is my cousin. We are grateful to yer grandfather for his intervention."

"Then Rory MacDunn is your uncle?" Gideon shook his head. "He's a good man. I'm glad the truth came out about the sheep."

"My cousin was in Dunderave when Craigg was caught in his lies," added Lachlan. "I imagine he liked the *scunner* less than me."

"I certainly don't trust the seedy shaver," he agreed. "It's hard to believe Lissie is related to him."

Lachlan grinned. "Ye can choose yer friends, but yer stuck with family."

Someone yelled from the courtyard that the bride had arrived. Maeve took Gideon's arm, and they moved to the entrance. Before they left the hall, Kirstine noted that he had attached Lissie to his other arm.

"May I?" asked Lachlan, extending his arm. She placed his fingers on his.

Outside, Nessie waited in a wagon, her cheeks glowing in her muslin rose gown. Her shining, dark hair fell loose over her shoulders, crowned with a ringlet of pink flowers.

"Right foot forward for good luck," someone yelled.

"Yer father hated these old wives' tales. I've almost forgotten some of them," she heard Maeve tell Gideon as the girl stepped down with the correct foot.

A piper led the procession to the kirk, followed by neighbors who sprinkled a trail of flower petals, the groom, and then Lachlan escorting the bride. The bagpipes serenaded the party as they stopped at the front steps. The men were splendid in their tartans with dress sporrans and glinting dirks, hair clean and shining, beards trimmed or faces shaved. The women wore their best satin or silk dresses or earasaids, plaids over their shoulders or across their chest, depending on their station.

At the ancient kirk door, Reverend Robertson welcomed the couple. Hamish gave Nessie a sheaf of wheat, and she gave him a piece of woven cloth, representing their promise to each other to provide for their home. Next, the couple exchanged a dagger and a bible.

"This shows his physical pledge and her spiritual pledge to defend their home," the reverend spoke to the assembly. The guests crowded into the small church. Near the altar, Lachlan's sword hissed as he unsheathed it to make a circle around the couple. As he did so, the couple said in unison,

"The Mighty Three, my protection be, encircle me,
You are around my life, my love, my home.
Encircle me, O sacred three, the Mighty Thee."

Reverend Robertson finished the ceremony and presented the couple to the crowd. "You may kiss the bride." Hamish took Nessie's hands in his and stared at her for a long moment. Then he dipped his head, brushed his lips lightly across her mouth, and leaned his forehead against hers. Kirstine dabbed at her eyes with her knuckle, so happy for the young couple who had come so close to losing one another.

Aye, Brodie, it's our turn next.

⇒⇒⇒✠⇐⇐⇐

BRODIE SCANNED THE Great Hall. Never had he washed and dressed so fast. He had helped his pain-in-the-arse sister deliver the calf, and now he wanted Kirsty, a meal, and some good scotch. In that order. Maybe the scotch first. It was a cèilidh, after all.

The great hall glittered with hundreds of flickering candles. Peigi had ordered the chandeliers lit to fill the center of the room with blazing light for eating and dancing. The wall torches, also ablaze, cast dancing shadows around the perimeter. The banners of allied clans hung from the aged stone walls, along with medieval tapestries bought or made by previous castle residents. To the right, in the far corner, an elevated platform held the musicians. To the left, a dais was set up for the clan chief and his family or honored guests. When his grandmother refurnished this space, she managed to blend the old with the new seamlessly.

Brodie loved events in the ancient hall. He could feel his ancestors in this room, feel their joy and outrage, their hope and despair. It was as if they guided him, along with his grandfather, to honor this clan, these people, and help bring them not only prosperity but contentment. He looked up at the brass chandeliers purchased less than fifty years ago. Aye, Peigi understood the need to maintain tradition yet move forward in an ever-changing world.

He finally spotted Kirsty at a table with Rory MacDunn.

For the love of saints! His blood heated at the sight.

She was stunning in a midnight blue gown, layered with a sheer silvery material that shimmered as she reached for her cup. Her hair was swept back, fiery curls cascading over a slender neck. When had she gone from bonny lass to seductive and enchanting? His gaze lingered on the creamy mounds shown off by the neckline, then moved up to her full lips. His mouth watered. His appetite had changed course. Her dark eyes sparkled in the candlelight and she nodded.

On the dais, Calum stood, a glass held high. To the right of his grandparents were the original guests of honor, his aunt and cousin, and to their left was the newly married couple. Brodie's chest swelled at the image of that poor girl, not only escaping a cruel father, but finding a loving husband. The good Lord could not keep evil from the world, but he gave people ways to fight against it if they listened and had the courage.

"A toast to family, to beginnings,"—Calum's eyes looked up—"to endings. May God keep us within his sight. Long live the clan MacNaughton!"

"Long live the clan MacNaughton!" echoed the guests.

Then he passed the two-handled quaich down the table. The young couple filled the ancient vessel with whiskey and moved to the table below. Hamish gave it to his father, who took a drink then offered it to Lissie's father, who stood in place of Nessie's father. The couple then drank from the cup, and the hall resounded with loud cheers.

The quaich was a family heirloom. It was used when the bride and groom came from different clans, the double handle representing the joining of the families. A tradition as old dirt, as his grandmother would say. Brodie embraced the old rituals. Such customs bound their people together, gave them a common ground that transcended class or title. It was a comforting thought—that one belonged no matter his birth.

"May I join ye?" he asked after Hamish and Nessie had returned to the dais.

Kirstine grinned. "I'd like that."

Platters filled with venison and pork, tender from cooking all day, were passed along the trestles. Well-seasoned vegetables, mashed tatties, warm bread, and freshly churned butter were set out in bowls and crockery. The wine and ale flowed. At the dais, Calum again called for their attention as the ceremonial platter of haggis was set before him. He stood, slid a polished blade through the boiled sheep's stomach, and sliced it open. The skin split, ground offal, oats and grains spilling out in a steaming heap. The spicy aroma filled the air and a round of *hurrahs* rang out.

His mother called for him just as the fiddler let out a warning note for the music to begin. "Excuse me," he said to those seated nearby. He stood and whispered to Kirsty, "Save me a dance?"

She nodded, and he felt her eyes on his back as he walked away. It would be tonight. He would ask her again, and this time, she would say yes. Brigid had finally confessed, desperate for his help with the calving: Kirsty was following Glynnis's instructions and was anxious to marry him. Much to his surprise, Brodie had not minded his mother's little plot and understood. He had not appreciated Kirsty before. Loved her, yes, but he'd taken her for granted. Brodie smiled, his determination as strong as the scotch.

But when he returned, the first set had begun, and Kirsty's seat was empty. He searched the crowd and saw her beginning a set with MacDougal. Jealousy churned in his gut. Unfounded, granted, but the longer he watched the two, the more it roiled. She knew he would be right back. MacDougal would have asked her for another dance.

"Brodie," said a soft voice at his elbow. "I've never thanked ye for helping that day my grandmother was ill."

"I was happy to do what I could." He looked down at Mairi, soft green eyes full of admiration, her coppery waves spilling down her back. "Ye look bonny tonight, Mairi."

"Thank ye." She blushed, then her gaze fell on Kirsty and Mac-Dougal. "Would ye like to dance the next set? I believe it's a reel."

The music had ended. MacDougal bowed to Kirsty and offered his arm. They moved between the dancers, walking back to the table. The older man leaned down and said something in her ear, and she nodded, then laughed. Brodie ground his teeth and took Mairi's hand, weaving toward the next set of dancers.

As the two couples passed, MacDougal nodded. Brodie glared. Kirsty rolled her eyes.

Mairi planted her feet. "Enough!" She crossed her arms. "Brodie MacNaughton, I'm no' dancing with a mon so he can send daggers across the room at the woman he loves. Kirstine MacDunn, shame on ye for making this poor mon all Friday-faced over ye."

MacDougal grinned. "Miss Mairi, would ye care to dance with me?"

"I'd love to, Liam." She cast a disgusted look at both of them.

Brodie stared at his shoes, then Kirsty. She peeked up at him through her lashes.

"Mairi's right," Kirsty murmured as someone jostled her from the back and pushed her against Brodie.

"Aye". He inhaled the scent of heather floating from her hair. "Shall we join them?"

"I thought ye'd never ask," she said with the sweetest smile.

"Minx," he whispered in her ear before he took her hand.

The fast-paced reel began in a circle, all participants holding hands. They split off into four lines, connected at the center, and moved in a clockwise direction but not with hands held. No, the dancers put their arms around each other's waist and twirled, which is why Brodie liked the reel. His palm cradled the curve of her hip through the thin muslin. She clung to him as the steps quickened. It was a teasing dance, their bodies pushed together from the momentum of the spinning, then separated. And then the clasping and whirling began all over again.

When the set ended, they were panting. Her chest rose and fell, her mouth slightly parted. If they were alone right now, he'd have kissed her. She seemed to read his mind.

"I need some fresh air." She waved her hand in front of her face like a fan.

But each time they tried to slip out of the hall, a guest stopped them. Lachlan appeared, a grin on his face. "It seems ye have come to yer senses," he said to Brodie before turning to Kirsty. "Would ye do me the honor of a dance?"

Brodie sighed, resigned. It was a cèilidh, after all.

An hour later, he led Kirsty across the courtyard and down the slight hill to the stable. The garden would have others enjoying fresh air and shadowed corners.

"Where are we going?" she asked.

"Where there's no one to interrupt us." He turned left at a mounting block. Brodie pulled her into the shadows of a small shed. She came willingly, her soft body pressed to his, her mouth upturned for a kiss. Who was he to make her wait?

His hand skimmed her cheek, then stroked her neck. He dipped his head, brushed her lips with his, and he was lost. His tongue plundered her mouth as desire seared through his core. Her hands threaded his hair. He cupped her bottom and lifted her, fitting her into him. She gasped, her nails dragging down the back of his neck.

"I love ye, Kirsty MacDunn," he growled in her ear, setting her feet back on the ground. His doubted his control if they continued. Their last time together in the pines had played over and over in his head the past two weeks.

"I love ye too." She pulled back just enough to look at him. "Will ye ask me tonight?"

"I will. And ye'll say yes."

"Ye're that sure?"

"Aye, Brigid told me." He grinned. "The jig is up."

"What exactly did she say?"

"That ye were ready to forgive right away, but my mother came up with a plan to teach me a lesson." Maybe not exactly what Brigid said. "And that ye yearned for me and was afraid I'd no' ask ye again. So, I'll put ye out of yer misery." Maybe he added that last part.

"Ye'll put me out of my misery?" Kirsty stepped back, her hands on her hips. "Ye can say that to me with a straight face?"

Bloody hell.

"Weel, ye'll be waiting until tomorrow then."

Kirsty gave him a wicked grin, stretched onto her tiptoes, and gave him a long kiss. Her hands trailed down his waistcoat as she pushed away from him.

"Brodie!" a voice called out.

Brigid was peering inside the stable. "Brodie, where are ye? Grand-da is asking for ye."

"Ye've been saved by a call of duty." He tipped Kirsty's chin up and gave her a quick kiss. "Ye may want to fix yer hair before ye return."

Her hands flew to chignon. "Go, I'll make myself presentable and meet ye back inside."

Brodie tipped her chin and gave her a kiss. Before the night ended, they would once again be betrothed. Better yet, handfasted. Any more arguments would be settled living under the same roof. Better yet, a bed canopy.

CHAPTER SEVENTEEN
Love Held Hostage

B RIGID TROTTED ALONG beside him as they returned to the castle. "What's so important?" he asked when they were almost to the courtyard.

"Grandda just said to find ye, and meet him near the copse in the garden." His sister grasped his arm. "Something has happened. I've no' seen Lachlan or Gideon either."

He nodded and turned from the castle entrance to go around the back. "Let me ken when ye find out," she called after him.

He found Calum at the far end of the garden, a large plaid on his lap. "There ye are. I need yer help to remove a body." His grandfather rose and headed toward the small wood.

"A what?" Brodie wondered if he'd drank too much. "Of an animal?"

"No, unfortunately. It seems Ross Craigg has revenge on his mind. Gideon and Lissie had taken some fresh air. She thought she heard a child cry in the dark and chased after it, Gideon following. Craigg was hiding with a hired thug, who grabbed Lissie." Calum paused at a clearing, and Brodie saw the body lying on the ground. "Lachlan heard her scream, thank God. Gideon killed the ruffian. Yer brother ran his sword through Craigg's side, but he got away."

"Is Lissie hurt?" He tried to digest this information. Going from sweet kisses to murder was a bit boggling.

Calum shook his head. "Bruised a bit, as is Gideon. They're both with Lachlan, who took a dagger in the leg from that bloody traitor. By God, the mon has pushed me too far."

"He's trying to sabotage the wedding?" It didn't make sense to wait until after the vows had been spoken.

His grandfather shook his head. "Worse than that. The mon is out for blood. If Lachlan hadna been there, Craigg would have killed Gideon, and possibly Lissie."

"The feckin' swine," rasped Brodie. "He's mad as a March hare."

"And needs to be skinned like one. He wants justice? By God, justice he shall have."

"Ye want me to find him, then?" Brodie's rage settled like a rock in his belly.

"No' till first light. Yer grandmother doesna want Nessie and Hamish to ken yet, no' on their wedding night. So, this will stay quiet until tomorrow." Calum ran a hand over his face. "First, we need to move the corpse so none of the guests stumble on it."

"Aye, we dinna need a posse of drunks on the moors at night," agreed Brodie. They wrapped the dead man in the plaid and carried him to the tool shed. "He canna go far with a hole in his gut."

"I dinna want ye out there alone. He may have more paid hooligans with him. Maybe we'll get lucky, and he'll be dead by dawn." His grandfather let out a long breath. "I need to get inside. If anyone asks, Lachlan and Gideon shared a bottle and are sleeping it off. Lissie retired early."

He nodded. "I'll fetch Mrs. MacDunn for Lachlan."

"No need. Enid is bandaging him and probably poured enough down his throat to make his sleep for a day." Calum thumped him on the back. "Go find yer woman and act as if nothing has happened. We're lucky there is only one casualty."

Brodie understood. The more people who knew, the harder it would be to keep quiet. Nessie had lived through hell in her short life. That bloody devil would not steal her happiness, not on her wedding night He followed his grandfather back into the great hall, skimming the hall for the silvery shimmer of Kirsty.

"What did ye find out?" Brigid asked from behind. "And dinna tell me 'nothing'."

"Craigg tried to cause trouble. It's been handled, though. Have ye seen Kirsty?"

She shook her head. "No' since she left with ye earlier. There's Mrs. MacDunn. I'll ask her." His sister dodged between the guests.

He watched the older woman shake her head and point toward the entrance. Mr. MacDunn joined them, shrugging his shoulders.

Brigid returned, worry in her deep blue eyes. "They've no' seen her either and her mother has looked about. She hoped Kirsty was still outside with ye."

"I've no' seen her since ye fetched me back to the castle. She should have been returned by now." Foreboding shot down Brodie's spine. "I have to find her. Tell Grandda where I've gone. He'll understand."

Heading to the stable, he broke into a jog. Sweat beaded on his forehead. *Where are ye Kirsty, love?* The question echoed in his brain. He'd find her. And never let her go.

»»»✦«««

KIRSTINE SMOOTHED HER stray curls as best she could. She smiled and licked her lips, where the taste of whisky still lingered from Brodie's kiss. When he asked her again, later tonight, she would say yes. She began to hum and twirled herself around as she slowly made her way toward the stable. The night air was cool on her skin, but she was in no hurry to return to the crowded hall. Kirstine wanted to savor this moment, this flash in time when the universe came together and all was right in her world.

Aagh.

She paused in mid-spin. Was that a groan?

It came again.

"Who's there?" she called out. Another soft moan coming from behind the barn. She pulled her shawl over her shoulders and moved toward the shadows. A horse snuffled. Perhaps it was an animal? She'd investigate and fetch Brigid if needed. Squinting into the dark meadow, she asked again. "Are ye hurt?"

A hand clamped over her mouth, wet and sticky, and she recognized the iron-like taste of blood.

"Aye, lass." His breath was hot and rancid against her cheek. Ross Craigg pressed her back against his chest, his arm like a vise around her waist. "We'll mount my horse together, ride to yer cottage, and ye'll doctor my gash. Then I'll be on my way."

He must be the reason Brodie had been called away. Had Brodie inflicted the wound or someone else? Had Craigg hurt anyone before he'd been attacked?

She shook her head and struggled against his hold. She doubled over, trying to kick at him, but her soft leather shoes made no impact except for a grunt of pain.

"I have a loaded pistol. If ye dinna come quietly, whoever ye alert will find a bullet in their brain." His lips moved against her skin; his hand squeezed her face. She gagged against the pervading odor. "Tell me ye understand."

She nodded, panic freezing her limbs. *Stay calm. Think!* ordered her brain.

"Put yer hands on the saddle and dinna move," he ordered.

Kristine's forehead rested against the saddle. The horse's soft breathing sent white puffs into the chilly evening air. Craigg's free hand fumbled with the ribbon at her waist and sheer terror sucked the breath from her lungs. She inhaled deeply, relieved when he wrapped it around her wrists. "If ye try to run while I bind ye, I'll shoot ye in the back. There'll be plenty of time to reload before yer hero finds ye."

She nodded and closed her eyes while he knotted the ribbon, winced at the satin digging into her tender skin. The steel barrel poked her ribs, and she scrambled into the saddle. Looking down, she saw the blood seeping through his coat. *Sweet Mary!* she thought as Craigg heaved himself behind her and kicked the horse into a gallop.

Kirstine took a deep breath to clear her mind. She would tend his wound, and he would leave. Ross Craigg would become a distant memory for all of them. She prayed for strength and blinked back tears. This man fed on weakness and fear. Kirstine refused to give him that power over her.

When they reached the cottage, Charlie's dark form ambled from the blackhouse. He stopped several yards from the horse and gave a soft warning growl. "Stay!" she ordered the hound, and he lay down with a soft whine. Craigg would have no compunction about shooting her dog. Sliding to the ground, Kirstine ran to Charlie and gave him a reassuring rub.

"If the beast even snarls, I'll shoot it."

"He's well trained and will do as I say. Charlie is also an excellent lookout and will let us ken if anyone approaches." She thought of Brodie and her parents. They would be frantic by now. "Let's get ye inside, so I can take a look at the damage."

"I'll stay right here where I can see who comes for me." He sat down heavily and leaned against the cottage, next to the door. Waving his gun with a grunt, he motioned her inside.

Kirstine rummaged in the pantry for the powder of cleaver, whisky, honey, then to the sitting room for needle, thread, rags, and winding cloth. When she returned, his eyes were closed. Could she run?

"Dinna consider escape until ye've doctored me," he mumbled.

With a sigh, she knelt beside him and concentrated on maintaining a steady hand. He had removed his coat and pulled up his shirt to reveal the deep laceration in his side. "I need to get some water from the well to clean this."

Before she could rise, he had her wrist in an iron grip. "Use the whisky."

"Fine, but it will hurt," she warned.

"It already hurts."

Kirstine poured the alcohol over the wound, and he let out a blood-curling screech, then whimpered softly while she cleaned it with a cloth. The man beat defenseless women but whined like a baby when pain was inflicted on him. Her lip curled in disgust.

"I could give ye some laudanum to ease the discomfort," she offered.

"Do ye think I'm addlepated? Just finish."

She sprinkled the powder over the wound and waited until the bleeding stopped. Threading the needle, Kirstine poked it into his skin and cringed at the pathetic keening. The seven-year-old boy with the broken arm last summer had been braver. Craigg's wails provoked the dog into low rumbles, and she had to hush Charlie several times before she finished. Her hands no longer trembled, her mind focused on finishing the task and sending the scoundrel on his way.

"How did this happen?" Perhaps she could distract him with conversation and find out if everyone was fine.

"I took retribution, or tried to." He grunted as she pulled him forward and wrapped the bandage around his back. "Had the young widow and lured the English grandson into the wood. If I'd shot him right away, my hired help wouldna be dead."

"Gideon killed a mon?" She remembered meeting him that afternoon. A handsome, polite man. Her stomach quaked. "And then ye shot him?"

"That feckin' Lachlan snuck up and ran me through. Lost a good dagger in his leg first, though."

"All of this because yer daughter married my cousin?"

He sneered. "The MacNaughton will understand I'm my own mon, no' bowing to anyone's orders. He's lorded over my family and pushed me around since my da died. Nessie was too much."

Kirstine pushed away and stood. Relief washed over her. No one had been hurt, save for a ruffian. Craigg would flee the Highlands, and she would find Brodie.

Ross struggled to his feet. "Help me onto my horse," he ordered. "Then I only have one last chore before I bid ye goodbye."

"She's done enough, ye stinking blaggard."

Brodie stood in the shadows of the yard. Her heart hammered at the sight of him, just as an arm pressed against her neck.

"Stand down, MacNaughton, or I'll blow her bonny little head to bits," Craigg rasped, holding the end of the long barrel under Kirstine's chin.

Charlie growled and slunk toward the horse.

"Down," Kirsty ordered in a quivering voice. She'd been so close. If Brodie had been a few minutes later…

"I'll no' let ye hurt her, Craigg. We both ken ye'd have shot her before ye left. That was yer plan, eh?" Brodie spoke in a calm, almost conversational tone. "The satisfaction of taking something from the MacNaughton. He's taken enough from yer family."

"Ye dinna ken the half of it." His arm tightened around her neck. "It was a good plan. Killing his grandson and the poor young widow under his nose. He'd never hold his head so high again. Instead, I had to settle for yer *betrothed*."

"Ye needed her first, though," Brodie continued, moving slowly forward.

Kirstine swallowed. She would have helped him onto the horse, and he would have shot her as he rode away. A wave of nausea rolled over her.

Concentrate! Help Brodie save ye!

Brodie's gaze locked with hers. His eyes made the slightest movement toward Charlie, then the fingers of his right hand wiggled. She glanced down at his right calf and saw the dirk he kept always kept there. He had a plan. If Charlie was on her right, she had to pitch to the left. She nodded and hoped, if things went awry, that he saw the love in her eyes.

"If ye let her go, I'll make sure no one follows until dawn."

"Dinna move another step." The hammer on the flintlock clicked.

"Dion!" bellowed Brodie, ordering the dog to defend as he pulled the blade and flung it forward.

The deerhound vaulted forward, and Kirstine leapt to the side. Craigg's arm jerked up to ward off the snarling dog, and the gun went off, just as the dirk landed in the saddle, just missing Craigg. Then Brodie sank to his knees with a curse.

"No!" she screamed and scrambled to him. A tremor ripped through her body. Fear squeezed her heart; she couldn't draw in a breath. Behind her, Craigg kicked at the hound as he struggled onto his horse. "Charlie, come!"

Kirstine fell to her knees beside Brodie. "Please don't die, please don't die," she panted over and over, her fingers searching for the wound.

"It grazed my arm and knocked me off balance. Ye'll no' get rid of me that easily." He sat up, scowling at the retreating figure. "The mon must have the devil riding on his shoulder."

Tears streamed down her cheek. She threw her arms around him, sobbing against his chest.

Brodie pulled her onto his lap and stroked her back. "Shhh, now, love," he murmured. "Ye're safe now." He chuckled at the sudden *thumping*. "I think yer other hero wants some thanks."

Kirstine wiped away her tears and hugged the deerhound, burying her wet cheeks in his wiry coat. "I love ye so."

"Me or the hound?"

"Both," she giggled, relief making her giddy.

"Then marry me." His hand cupped her cheek, his eyes dark as a stormy ocean. "Make yer promise to me, Kirsty." He kissed her, a soft whisper of a kiss. A gentle declaration of love.

"Yes," she said with a watery smile, letting the tears fall again.

"Up with ye then. Ye'll need to doctor one more mon tonight."

But when she turned to go into the cottage, he stopped her. "Wait," he said, turning her around so her back was to him. His fingers laced through her hair, and the curls fell against her neck.

"Turn around, love."

Kirsty watched as he looped the hair ribbon into a knot, took her finger, and placed the knot over their joined hands.

"A handfasting?" A slow smile turned up her lips. "It's no' legal."

"We'll still have a ceremony at the kirk, but this assures me there will be no more catastrophes between now and then."

"Aye, then, a handfasting it will be."

Brodie tipped her chin. "In the joining of hands and the fashion of this knot, so our lives are bound, one to another."

"May this knot remain tied for as long as love shall last," Kirstine whispered, fearing her voice would crack. The love in her heart for this man would fill a loch. "May this cord draw our hands together in love, never to be used in anger."

"May the vows we have spoken never grow bitter in our mouths."

Together they finished, "May it be granted that what is done before God, may not be undone."

"And now, I kiss the bride." He scooped her into his arms.

"Brodie, yer wound," she cried, but not letting go of his neck.

"Ye're all the medicine I need, Kirsty." He pressed his lips to hers, the gentleness replaced with need and desire. "Ye're all I'll ever need."

EPILOGUE

The Allusiveness of Love

February 1820
MacNaughton Castle

"WHEN DOES BRIGID leave for London?" asked Kirsty. "Ye ken she's refusing to cooperate once she's there. Says she'll be the 'Terror of the *Ton*' if she's forced to go."

"I'll talk to her."

"As her future chief or her brother?" Kirsty raised an eyebrow, then slowly pulled the strings to her chemise. A wicked grin curved her lips.

"Both," Brodie replied.

His grandfather had finally agreed—while they had scoured the Highlands for Ross Craigg—that Brodie was a better choice to lead the clan. "When I decide to step down," Calum had clarified. It still rankled that they'd never found the traitor Craigg. Though his wife and daughter didn't mourn his loss.

Brodie lay on the bed, bare as the day he was born, propped against the bolsters. His gaze lingered on his wife as she slowly removed her clothes. They had been married last October, and his love for her, his passion for her had only grown. He watched Kirsty undress and decided this was his favorite part of the evening. Alone and discussing their day, naked. He moaned as her shift pooled on the floor, and the vixen sauntered toward him. She laughed as his manhood swelled, running a finger up the length and over the tip. His ardor for her never diminished; the sight of her affected him every time. Every. Single. Time.

He grabbed her and flipped her body beneath him. "I'm no' concerned with my sister right now," he growled. He nibbled her ear lobe, then left a trail of kisses down her neck and across her collarbone. She had such a lovely neck. "And soon, she'll no' be yer concern either."

He cupped one breast and rubbed the pink tip until it pebbled, licking and then sucking the other. She wriggled beneath him, sending fire through his core. His mouth slowly eased down her stomach, to the soft skin just above her mound, while his hands continued their caresses.

"Brodie," she gasped. "Love me."

"Aye, right." He grinned as he parted the soft petals of her womanhood. His tongue found her secret spot, circling it, pulling it into his mouth until it hardened. His finger slipped inside and out again, her hips following the rhythm. He loved to watch her, the ecstasy on her face as release claimed her. Kirsty cried out, grasping his hair as her body rocked with tremors of pleasure.

Brodie moved over her and entered her slick passage, sinking his staff in deep with a loud groan. He stilled, gave her time to adjust to his member, and gain control of his hunger. Her hands roamed up and down his back. His mouth covered hers, their tongues dueling as he plunged into her, feeling the muscles tighten then relax.

"Brodie, oh God, Brodie!" She arched into him.

His thrusts came faster and more urgent, the desire spiraling, then bursting in an all-consuming release. He threw back his head, and the shout bounced off the ceiling as collapsed on top of her.

"I love ye, Brodie MacNaughton," Kirsty whispered into his ear.

"But ye really need to learn to be more quiet."

He rolled off her and pulled her close, skimming her bare hips with his fingertips. She kissed his neck, and he sighed, waiting for his heart to slow. "Why? We're the only ones on this floor. They canna hear us below."

She gave him a wicked smiled. Her finger traced circles on his chest. "No, but ye may wake the bairn when it comes."

He blinked. "Ye're with child?"

Kirsty nodded. "Aye, ye randy goat. There'll be a wee Brodie next fall."

Brodie sat up against the bolsters and pulled her onto his lap. "Just when I think I canna love ye more, ye surprise me again."

Love was an allusive faery, he had decided, dancing around and in front of him, surrounding him in a cocoon of tenderness and trust. A warm breath on his cheek, a random touch in the middle of the day, a shared look that no one else would understand. Kirsty's love had always been a part of him, intimated and whispered, waiting for him to listen. He kissed her soft lips, his hand spread across her belly, and thought of what he might have missed. It had taken an entire clan, but he had finally heeded the subtle call.

THE END

About the Author

Bestselling and award-winning author Aubrey Wynne is an elementary teacher by trade, champion of children and animals by conscience, and author by night. She resides in the Midwest with her husband, dogs, horses, mule, and barn cats. Obsessions include wine, history, travel, trail riding, and all things Christmas. Her books have received the Golden Quill, Aspen Gold, Heart of Excellence, and the Gayle Wilson Award of Excellence.

Aubrey's first love is medieval romance but after dipping her toe in the Regency period in 2018 with the *Wicked Earls' Club*, she was smitten. This inspired her spin-off series *Once Upon a Widow*. In 2020, she will launch the Scottish Regency series *A MacNaughton Castle Romance* with Dragonblade Novels.

Find Aubrey
Website: aubreywynne.com
Facebook: facebook.com/magnificentvalor
Twitter: @aubreywynne51
Instagram: Aubreywynne51

Subscribe to Aubrey's newsletter for new releases, exclusive excerpts, and free stories:
Newsletter: www.subscribepage.com/k3f1z5
Facebook Reading Group:
facebook.com/groups/AubreyWynnesEverAfters

Made in the USA
Monee, IL
08 April 2024

56573270R00105